MARTINE

Just what I had been afraid of, he was good to lie against. Damn those shoulders. And I liked putting my head against his chest which was even broader without clothes than it had seemed all tucked into a suit. I kept trying to tell myself that I was making love to a married man, but the married part kept eluding me, and all I kept thinking about was the man . . .

BLOCKBUSTER FICTION FROM PINNACLE BOOKS!

THE FINAL VOYAGE OF THE S.S.N. SKATE   (17-157, $3.95)
by Stephen Cassell
The "leper" of the U.S. Pacific Fleet, SSN 578 nuclear attack sub
SKATE, has one final mission to perform—an impossible act of
piracy that will pit the underwater deathtrap and its inexperienced
crew against the combined might of the Soviet Navy's finest!

QUEENS GATE RECKONING   (17-164, $3.95)
by Lewis Purdue
Only a wounded CIA operative and a defecting Soviet ballerina
stand in the way of a vast consortium of treason that speeds toward the hour of mankind's ultimate reckoning! From the best-
selling author of THE LINZ TESTAMENT.

FAREWELL TO RUSSIA   (17-165, $4.50)
by Richard Hugo
A KGB agent must race against time to infiltrate the confines of
U.S. nuclear technology after a terrifying accident threatens to
unleash unmitigated devastation!

THE NICODEMUS CODE   (17-133, $3.95)
by Graham N. Smith and Donna Smith
A two-thousand-year-old parchment has been unearthed, un-
leashing a terrifying conspiracy unlike any the world has previ-
ously known, one that threatens the life of the Pope himself, and
the ultimate destruction of Christianity!

*Available wherever paperbacks are sold, or order direct from the
Publisher. Send cover price plus 50¢ per copy for mailing and
handling to Pinnacle Books, Dept.17-231, 475 Park Avenue
South, New York, N.Y. 10016. Residents of New York, New Jer-
sey and Pennsylvania must include sales tax. DO NOT SEND
CASH.*

Lovers

BY CARMEL BERMAN REINGOLD AND HARRY REINGOLD

PINNACLE BOOKS
WINDSOR PUBLISHING CORP.

PINNACLE BOOKS

are published by

Windsor Publishing Corp.
475 Park Avenue South
New York, NY 10016

First printing: July 1989

Printed in the United States of America

And for Hillel Black . . . who made us take that extra step.

Happiness will come . . . eventually. Meanwhile, give
a party.

From *Lenke's Journals (translation)*

CHAPTER I

Andy

That year I was a summer bachelor. Again. Oh boy! Let me tell you about summer bachelors. We see a lot of television. Eat quick meals. And if we're lucky, get to talk a lot of business with other summer bachelors. Maybe even see a porno movie.

Curiously, I didn't mind it. I even liked it. I missed the kids a little. But when the weekends came I was their hero. And the price of boredom was worth the quiet and peace I got living alone. That's one of the big problems of marriage, even a good one. A husband is almost never alone, not even for an hour. You get up in the morning, have breakfast with your family, go to work, come home, have dinner with the wife and kids. The kids go to sleep and you listen to your wife talk. Maybe television, and finally sleep. The next day breakfast and togetherness. At least in the summer I enjoyed a new routine.

I work for an ad agency, and summers are slow. Business is sluggish in the summer. Half the clients and half the agency are on vacation, and you can't find anyone to give you a yes or a no to a new idea. One afternoon I was sitting in my office, leafing through a trade magazine when Jim O'Donnell walked in. I should say Jim leaned into my office. Jim always looks as though he's on the run.

"What are you doing, Andy?" He glanced at my magazine. "You look as bored as I feel. You better come with me—I'm going to a party."

I looked at Jim warily. I had some idea about his parties.

"Come on. What else have you got to do? We'll have a few drinks, meet a few people."

With Jim translate *people* to *girls*.

"It's being given by the Latin American Tourist Council at the Plaza. I'll pick you up in half an hour." And he was gone.

Go to a party? I didn't really care. But Jim was right. I had nothing better to do. I like Jim; life and its problems rest lightly on his shoulders. He never seems to get angry or emotional about anything, and he's a good listener. Once in a while we'd get together for dinner. I liked listening to his adventures with women. Jim likes women, and he isn't too fussy—a good combination. He takes the craziest chances and gets away with them. Jim's married, with a couple of kids, too, but he always has plenty of time to play around. That summer he was having an affair with the agency president's secretary; that's what I mean about taking a crazy chance.

Jim and I got to the Plaza a few minutes after five,

and the place was already jammed. There was a reception desk with two very pretty Latin American girls. Dark complexion, smooth and firm, long dark hair, short skirts and bulging, prim white blouses. It was the hair that got me. I've got a thing for long hair.

"Name?" one of the girls asked me.

"Andy Lang."

She filled out a badge with my name and attached it to my lapel. She stood close and looked right in my eyes. It was going to be a nice party. We walked into the suite and another Miss Latin America handed me a glass of champagne. God, was it sweet. I made a face when I tasted it, and a girl standing next to me laughed. She had long, dark hair, too.

"Don't you like champagne?" she asked.

"Not really. Especially New York State champagne. It makes me burp a lot."

"They've got a bar," she said, pointing.

"Can I get you a drink?" I asked.

"I've got one, thanks. I don't mind New York State champagne."

"How about waiting here until I get one?" And I headed for the bar and my dependable dry vodka martini. When I came back, the girl was still there, and now she was talking to Jim and to another girl whom she introduced as Dee Dee.

Dee Dee. What a name. It sounds easy to remember, but I always have trouble with names like Binky and Dee Dee and Jay Jay. Jim was paying close attention to Dee Dee, which suited me just fine. I disliked her on sight. Short blond hair, sloppy clothes, and obvious. She was wearing a tailored blue suit, but there was nothing subtle about her. She wasn't wearing a blouse or a bra, and her jacket was half-buttoned. Jim was doing his best to impress her, but I could sense she was appraising him, and not listening. She seemed tough and a little unbathed, but that was Jim's problem.

I turned to the dark-haired girl. "Okay, now that we have our drinks, let's get the preliminaries over with. I'm Andy Lang, I work for an ad agency, I'm married, and I've got two kids."

Jim looked at me as though I were some kind of a nut. These girls had probably figured that we were both married. Why did I have to blurt it out like that? But Jim and I are different. I didn't want any misunderstandings. When I get involved in fun and games, that's all they are—fun and games. Jim would dangle promises in front of a girl to push the sexual adventure along. I wouldn't.

The dark-haired girl took another sip of champagne. She looked bored, and she kind of mimicked me when she said, "My name is Martine Lukas. And I went to Public School 189, and I've forgotten what I did on my last summer vacation, but I remember that I'm a free-lance writer. And not that anyone cares, but I'm not married, and I'm happily child-free."

I winced, and Dee Dee laughed. It wasn't a pleasant laugh, so I turned away from her, and pretending that I hadn't sounded like an idiot a few minutes before, I asked this Martine girl what kinds of things she wrote.

She shrugged. That question seemed to bore her, too. "Articles, books, cookbooks, celebrity interviews, fashion. Everything and nothing."

Well, at least she had stopped making fun of me. The cocktail chatter continued, and then we sat through

12

a film presentation which tried to convince us that Argentina was a combination of Venice, Paris, Switzerland, and Africa. A tourist's paradise.

They served a tableful of food after that, and the way everyone descended on that buffet, you'd think they were all just told this was going to be the last meal of their lives.

I looked at the picked-over shrimp and the once-again chicken wings. "Why don't we go out to dinner?"

Dee Dee was quick to answer yes for everybody. She grabbed Jim's arm, and the four of us headed away from the table and toward the door.

I can't say the dinner was especially interesting. Jim was busy giving Dee Dee his direct-eye-contact technique, and he ignored me and Martine. Martine had a quick answer to everything, but at least she was funny. That's another thing I'm a sucker for—funny women. I always figure that a girl who's funny has to be bright. What's the connection? I don't know. But that's my experience. I don't mean telling jokes. I've never known a good woman raconteur. But then I've never known a woman who tried. Martine was quick. I liked that.

She asked me about my kids, and I told her about them. I found out that her mother came from France and that she spoke French, and was a great cook. Later on, I found out that she lived on the East Side. That was when I took her home. She didn't invite me up, but that didn't bother me. It was late, and I wanted to get some sleep. It wasn't an exciting evening, but it was better than summer television.

CHAPTER II

Martine

It was summer—again. Summer, this girl's least favorite time. If you work in New York, you know that people call the days between Christmas and New Year's the silly season. But summer is more than silly, it's crazy time in New York. Business is slow, and people in my town figure that if we can't make money, maybe we can make each other.

That's how summer has hit me for a long time. And in New York summer craziness begins in February, with all the lemmings running around trying to arrange the summer, which is only four months away.

"Hey, listen, how would you like to take a quarter of this weekend share I have in a four-and-a-half-bedroom house in Fire Island?

"What does it mean? It means you can have my room every fourth weekend. It's a long season, so you'll have at least four weekends at the beach. Look, you never know who you'll meet out there. You can make great contacts that will last you all through next winter. Why, just last year . . ."

Just last year . . . this lucky girl met the Shah of Seventh Avenue. Very big in sealskin underwear. Just last year . . . this guy met this girl whose father is Mr. Breakstone. Yeah, Mr. Breakstone, the butter and sour-cream millionaire. And he married this Breakstone heiress . . . or the Sealtest heiress . . . or the Dannon heiress . . . the Haagen-Dazs heiress. What's the difference, which one? She was loaded!

But I don't want you to think that all these crazies are crazy only about money. We definitely run a class act here in New York. Money isn't everything. The idea is to meet people in the summer who will let you lay them in the winter. Or will lay you in the winter. Whichever.

And God forbid that Labor Day comes around and you haven't got anyone to go with to the latest films during that wonderful crispy fall, that divine, crystal-clear winter. Because if that happens, you get to do the whole number all over again, and you start signing up for the charters to St. Croix over Thanksgiving, Zermatt for Christmas, Acapulco for that bloody long Washington's Birthday weekend. And then there's always that godawful Club Med, if worst comes to worst. Above all, you can't be alone in the big city.

Admit that you're alone in New York, and you're admitting to failure. And if you're a failure, you might as well be dead.

You're a loner? We've all heard that one before. People who claim to be loners are just people who can't find anyone. No one wants them.

Now you know why I'm not crazy about summer. Too much running around, too many fixed smiles bracketing too many capped teeth, too many people saying, "Isn't this the best summer ever?" when their eyes tell you that summer is just a hotter brand of hell.

Of course, you do meet a different type of man in the summer. You meet the married bachelor. The Mr. Nice Guy who has taken a house for his wife and children on Fire Island, or in the Hamptons, or if he's really lucky, up in Martha's Vineyard. Why does Martha's Vineyard spell good luck? Because the poor bastards with wives and kids stashed on Fire Island or in the Hamptons have got to show up every weekend, but Martha's Vineyard provides a big bouquet of excuses. It's too far if you have a big meeting on Monday. And if the weather is bad, the planes don't take off. The Long Island Railroad always takes off. Its motto is: We take forever, but we get there.

Why do women go to Fire Island, or wherever, leaving their husbands on the loose Mondays through Fridays? They say it's for the good of the children. I say it's because they're just as bored with their husbands as their husbands are with them. Anything else is a lie, all the open marriage garbage notwithstanding. Listen, if you thought you owned a gem of purest ray serene, would you go handing it out to everyone who tried to cop a feel, or would you keep it pretty close to home? Okay, that's what I thought you'd say.

Anyway, summertime is when all the men who run for the 5:55 to Greenwich and the 5:42 to Scarsdale suddenly surface. And summer was when I met him.

The big public relations firms in New York are the ones who give the best parties, because they have the

17

most money. They take the suites at the Plaza or the Park Lane or the Regency or the St. Regis, and you are invited to a party in honor of the Spanish Olive Institute, or the Peanut Institute or the Sauerkraut Council (so help me). If those don't appeal to you, there are also the invitations from foreign countries who are trying to drum up tourist trade. If the invitation is from one of the oil countries, go—there will be lots of caviar.

Anyway, I didn't meet this guy I'm about to tell you about at the Saudi press party because my friend who used to handle that account is mad at me, so I no longer get invited for the caviar.

No, I met him at a party given by the Latin American Tourist Council. They invited a whole bunch of travel agents, some advertising people, and every member of the press they could contact. That's me—I'm a member of the press.

Have you ever heard of me? Probably not. I've got the kind of name that slips the mind easily. But you've probably read my articles. On travel, food, fashion, politics, children, marriage, divorce, cars, entertaining, whatever. Whatever makes me money.

Do I like press parties? Not too much, but as my mother is forever saying, You Never Know Who You're Going To Meet. Some of the people I've met, well, forget it. But don't put all parties down, because as my mother said, and this time she was right, amid all the tiny Latin Americans wearing the built-up heels was this North American, genuine New Yorker, who towered nicely above all the cute guys with melting Latin eyes who reached the level of my ear.

It isn't height that counts! It isn't looks that count!

It isn't money that counts! It's what the person has inside! You're certainly right, but meanwhile I like them on the tall side, and with the right amount of eyes and nose, and I think it's wrong to hate someone just because he's got money.

But back to this guy. What can I call him? No real names, please, all characters in this book are strictly fictitious. Sure, sure, from Juliet to Fagin to that nasty ex-wife who keeps reappearing in Philip Roth's books, show me a fictional character.

Anyway, his name was—and is—Andrew Lang. Come on, like the guy who wrote all those fairy tales? Sure, why not? Maybe I kissed this frog and he turned into a prince, who are you to say no?

Well, there I was with a glass of champagne—press parties are big on champagne—and I was talking to my good friend Dee Dee who was surveying the scene with what I've seen other writers call a jaundiced eye.

"No one," Dee Dee said. "Absolutely dreck."

"Give it a chance," I said. "Have an olive."

"An olive, hell, I'm having some of that lobster stuff."

"The mayonnaise looks as though it's turning. Have an olive, and then we'll go have dinner."

Dee Dee sighed. "I suppose you're right."

Every girl like me has to know a girl like Dee Dee. We're both on the same level of success, and that means that we have no worries about going to good restaurants and picking up our dinner checks. Dee Dee is a songwriter, and though you probably don't know her name either, you've also just as probably hummed along while Shirley Bassey or maybe Linda Ronstadt has sung her songs.

It was while Dee Dee was being pensive over an olive that these two guys ankled over. Ankled, not rushed. I always wear dark glasses which gives me a chance to look and not be looked at too closely. Of the two, I liked Andrew Lang best. He had this dark wavy hair, broad shoulders, and a nonsoft face. I've never liked cute, boyish types. Mid-thirties, I figured, and very broad shoulders. I said that. Well, I'm saying it twice, because I like broad shoulders.

The other guy was what I call the black Irish type, though an Irish guy I know says I'm using the phrase all wrong. Anyway, what I mean by black Irish is an Irish guy with jet black hair and blue eyes who looks as though he had a Spanish buccaneer ancestor somewhere in the background

I've set it all up for you, so you won't be surprised that Andrew Lang's friend's name was Jim O'Donnell. Nice-looking, in a tall, snaky way. One of the up-to-no-good guys who will try to maintain that boyish look into his foolish fifties. That type keeps forgetting that Mark Twain never let Huckleberry Finn get out of his teens.

But it was okay, because Dee Dee likes the up-to-no-good boyish type. As she says, "When I'm hungry I just want a quick lay. I don't want to get involved."

Anyway, it was all very pleasant for about sixty seconds or so. The usual What do you do? And what do *you* do? And everyone approves of everyone else because it's clear that we're all in about the same financial bracket.

That's nice, and that's also a smidge unusual, because married bachelors generally look for sweet little secretaries who are in their early twenties and who

20

are ready to be impressed with a good dinner and an account executive's credit card. And girls like me and Dee Dee generally look for presidents or at least financial officers of major companies. It's kind of interesting, but in this swift courtship dance meant to lead only to bed, the men look downward while the women look upward.

But this one night, the four of us started out kind of even, which made it a little easier on the nerves. No one was out to impress anyone, and whoever climbed into bed wouldn't have anyone special to brag about the next day.

I liked Andrew Lang. What did he say? Can't remember, not because it was forgettable, but because like the best kind of wit, it was quick, spontaneous, and seemingly unending.

That was the first sixty seconds, and then he had to spoil it all by blurting out, "I'm married, you know."

"He's married, you know," I said to Dee Dee.

Pretended shock. "The hell you say!"

"Andy, for God's sake." Boyish Jim felt his game was being spoiled, which cracked us up, me and Dee Dee, that is.

Andrew Lang did a quick recovery. "Are you girls busy? How about dinner?"

All charm again, but I was annoyed from before. Who asked him for the story of his life?

"Sorry—"

"No you're not," Dee Dee interrupted me. "What have you got to be sorry about? You haven't done anything—yet. Dinner, sure."

In the ladies' room—powder room—john—loo—

21

what do you like to call it? Dee says, "I'm tired of paying for my own dinner."

Sensible me: "Why? You've got the money."

"Just because."

I understood. Sometime not too long ago Dee Dee had been poor. This was before her songs were played as the background of all those spy movies. Once poor, always poor. Dee Dee rebelled about paying for her own dinners. Not that she paid for too many of them. There were these men winging in from Hollywood: record producers, movie producers, actors, all of whom wanted to take Dee Dee to dinner, and onward from there.

"Why bother?" I asked her.

"I get hungry," she said.

"For food?"

"For that, too."

That night, for me, it was just dinner, but Dee Dee and Huckleberry Finn Jimmy went on from the restaurant. They didn't make much of an excuse as they left me and Andrew Lang sipping stingers. The black Irishman was surprised, I could see that. He was getting what he wanted, but was disappointed that it had nothing to do with his seductive powers. Dee Dee thought he had a good body, and she was in the mood. That kind of ease always floors suburban men. At least, I figured he was a suburban man.

"Where does your friend live?" I asked Andy Lang.

"In Manhasset."

Yes. "And you?"

"On the West Side."

That might be a problem. A city boy. Suburban men were easier. They knew they had to work for what you

22

ave them, and if you gave them nothing, that was all ight too. They wanted the name rather than the game.

I fiddled with my drink, and I only half-listened to im. I wished I could be like Dee Dee, but my absotely unbreakable rule number one: Do Not Get Involved With Married Men, and any guy who tells you hat he's married one quick minute after he's met you s very married indeed. Too bad, those shoulders really oked good to me. Good to lean against, good to lie n . . .

I took the quick cold-water cure. I asked him about is children. That usually does it for me. Sure enough, e told me about his children. Earnestly, sincerely, and n detail. The older girl was the prettiest in the world. Vhy, when she was only eight months old. . . . And he younger girl had the curliest hair. People always sked, Why not let them model? But that was a terrible hing to do to kids.

A really nice guy, I decided. If I had a nice guy like hat, I wouldn't go off to Fire Island and leave him in New York, a cute sitting duck. It's all for the children. But how bad is New York for children? There are lots f parks and pools and plenty of air conditioning, and loesn't milk come with all the Vitamin A the body can ake? Well, never mind. This was A Married Man.

I started fussing with my lipstick. Time to go. I let im take me home. Just as far as Sam, the doorman.

"Can I see you again?" He had nice, warm brown yes, too.

"I'm sorry, but . . ."

"Can I call you? Look, you're a free-lance writer. My agency, sometimes we use free-lancers."

23

Use. Bad word that. Oh, don't be such a weigher and measurer of unconsidered trifles.

"Sure, you can call me. I'm in the book."

And that was that. Until next morning with Dee Dee on the phone.

"Well?" she asked.

"Nothing. And you?"

I could picture her shrug. "He looked better than he was." Yawn. "Better luck next time."

And that was how I met Andrew Lang.

CHAPTER III

Andy

Friday. Time to clean up my desk, leave the office a little early, go to Penn Station, and get the train to Bay Shore and the daddy boat to Fire Island to spend the weekend with my wife and two kids. That was the routine every Friday from May 31st to a week after Labor Day. Then on Sunday evening, like all the rest of the daddies, get the daddy boat and taxi to the rackety, noisy, dirty Long Island Railroad for the trip back to the city.

When I was a kid I used to go with my family or friends to the city beaches for a day. I'd wear my bathing suit under my clothes. Coming back at the end of the day was uncomfortable. I was still wearing my bathing suit plus a lot of sand. The older I got the more uncomfortable it seemed, so that by the time I was seventeen I stopped day trips to the beach.

Now I'd moved up in the world. I had a house by

the sea at Fire Island that I rented for the entire summer, and I could go out on weekends.

Fire Island is a sandbar off the coast of Long Island and a sexual legend propagated by writers who have nothing to write about. It was supposed to be a great place to meet lots of girls, get laid lots of times, orgies, everything.

When I first discovered Fire Island I thought it was the most beautiful place I had ever seen. The beaches weren't crowded on weekends, and during the week you could stand on stretches of the island and not see a single soul. All you saw was sand, ocean, dunes, scrub pine, and poison ivy. It was a city boy's dream come true.

Fire Island is where I first met Janet. She was weekending in a house rented by a group of singles, and I was in the house next door, part of another group. The houses were old, rambling, and not in very good condition, but they were spacious, with lots of bedrooms, and large groups rented them at outrageously inflated prices. As long as enough people shared a house, the rents were bearable.

It didn't take long before the folks at both houses discovered each other and got together for a party, and that's how I discovered Janet. She was nice-looking, with long, light brown hair, blue eyes, and a good figure. She was well-dressed, too, right out of Bergdorf's, elegant, expensive, and underplayed. I liked her style, and I told her so. She told me that she loved the beach and the water, and had grown up on Long Island, in Glen Cove where her parents had a house on Long Island Sound. She had learned to swim and sail as a child, she said.

26

I was impressed. I had never even been on a sailboat and was only a fair swimmer. Janet was different from the girls I had grown up with in New York City. She was suburban, self-assured, elegant and well-to-do. Her background was so different from mine that it took a lot of courage to ask her if she'd like to come for a walk on the beach. She said yes, and with our drinks in our hands we went for a stroll. It was a beautiful, starlit Saturday night in midsummer. We soon got rid of our drinks and held hands as we walked. The water was calm and I asked Janet if she wanted to go for a swim. She said that was a good idea, and we stripped and ran into the surf. The water was brisk but bearable. Janet seemed so free-spirited, so natural. I was falling in love.

We didn't make love that first night. The conditions were right, but all we did was kiss. It was sweet and not too urgent. I knew we would see each other again, and it didn't matter if I didn't score then.

After that first walk on the beach, I called Janet in New York on Monday and asked her to have dinner at my apartment. I left my office early and stopped at the fanciest take-out place in my neighborhood to buy things for dinner. Not that the food mattered. Janet and I had a drink, and then we decided that eating later was a better idea.

Our affair was off the ground and flying. I liked Janet's matter-of-fact manner about sex. She never started anything, but she didn't say no, either.

Occasionally she made dinner for me at her apartment, but we spent most of our time together at my place because she had a roommate who always seemed to be home.

While we were going around together I discovered

27

that Janet wasn't that much of an uptown girl after all.
Both she and her mother worked. Her father had been
wealthy, she said, but he ran off with another woman
and she hadn't seen him for years. She had dropped
out of college during her first year, and she had a job
that was okay but not the most exciting thing in the
world.

Janet wasn't all that different from the girls I had
grown up with, but it didn't matter. I thought we were
right for each other, and I asked her to marry me one
night after we had made love. To my surprise, she said
she wasn't sure. That's when she told me about this
guy she had been seeing for close to two years who had
suddenly decided to say goodbye to her just a few
months before we had met. She said she had to think
about my proposal.

Janet's hesitancy made me more eager than ever to
marry her. We were good in bed, we had fun, and
most of the guys I knew were already married. Janet
knew that I wasn't making a lot of money, but I assured her that my prospects were good.

Three days later Janet said yes, and we were married a couple of months later. We went to Bermuda for
our honeymoon, and the next summer we rented a
house on Fire Island.

No matter how my relations with Janet shifted,
changed from good to bad, I was drawn to that wonderful beach. But now, even that was changing. I felt
glum as I stood on the deck of the ferry as it approached Fire Island. I counted no fewer than thirty-
eight yelling, screaming, prancing, tanned and healthy
kids—my two among them—all shouting, "Daddy
Daddy . . ."

Janet was there too, dressed in a striped T-shirt and walking shorts. Somebody hated women when he invented walking shorts. The length is so indecisive. It makes all women look truncated and fat-legged.

Barbara and Diane were in the ubiquitous red wagon. Everybody on Fire Island has to have a red wagon. It's the only way to transport anything. The streets aren't paved, there are narrow boardwalks, and no cars are allowed. So when you go to the food market in town you need a wagon. It's also used to pull kids around, especially the smaller ones.

As soon as I got off the boat Barbara and Diane leaped all over me, demanding I pick them up, hugging me and obviously glad to see me, with no restraint. Janet waited patiently, half-frowning. She has a good frown; it lets you know right away something is bothering her. I wasn't sure she was so glad to see me. Finally with the two kids wriggling in my arms but under control, I leaned over to Janet and we kind of kissed.

I felt good holding the two squirming bodies. Barbara was kind of round—a little overweight, I was told. But I thought she was simply delicious. Diane was firm and just right, according to the doctor. Barbara and Diane competed shamelessly for my exclusive attention, while Janet stood by with her arms crossed, waiting.

"How was your week?" I asked, wrestling with the kids.

"I'm glad you asked. Diane has a cold. Ran a small fever for a couple of days and was a total pain in the ass. I couldn't leave the house and Barbara didn't like being stuck in the house, so she was a pain too.

29

Mommy this and mommy that. I thought I'd go crazy. I'm glad you came. You can have them for a couple of days."

Daddy's role in life defined: relieve mommy from her week of drudgery at the beach.

We walked back to the house, me pulling the wagon with the kids in it.

"If you want a drink," Janet said, "the bottles are on the sideboard and the ice is in the refrigerator. While you're at it, make me one, too. And we're having an early dinner, the Greens have invited us to their house. They're having some people over."

The Greens are friends we see all year round. They had been friends of Janet's before we were married. They live in the city, on the West Side too, and were neighbors of ours on Fire Island. It seemed to me our whole circle of friends and acquaintances—indeed, the whole West Side—moved in lockstep. We were all about the same age, made about the same income, all had college educations, averaged 2.3 children, came from the same background. Had apartments in the city and a summer house on Fire Island. Sociologists would find us a bore.

It's like the guy who discovers he's just like all his friends, associates, neighbors. Feels he didn't go to Harvard to be like everybody else. So he gives up his work, his family. Spends all his money trying to find the meaning of life and why he isn't different from anybody else.

He's finally sent to the wisest man in the world, the Dalai Lama in Tibet, and asks him the meaning of life. The Dalai Lama, reputedly at least one hundred and twenty years old, says, "Life is like a fountain," at which point the man cries out, "Is that all? I've traveled this far, given up everything, my wife, my family, friends, I'm crippled and old and all you say is life is like a fountain . . ."

The Dalai Lama looks bewildered at this sudden assault and questioning of his wisdom, and says, "You mean life is *not* like a fountain?"

We got to the Greens' house. The usual West Side crowd was there, fashionably dressed in designer jeans and old shirts. The usual round of vodka-tonics and wine spritzers, and some old jokes with a few new ones. The buffet dinner was laid out, and we all helped ourselves and sat down balancing plates on our laps.

The men told their wives, and anyone else who would listen, about all the big and little things that had happened in the city during the week.

"I made a pitch for this new package goods account . . ."

"I told Brady that I don't care if he is the hospital administrator, I still say that's no way to run a hospital . . ."

I was eating my pasta-with-pesto and not paying too much attention when I heard Hal Green say:

"Hey, guys, you know who I ran into on Fifth Avenue just yesterday? Dick Templeton."

There was a half second of silence. Almost everyone in the room was an old friend of Janet's, and all those friends knew that Dick Templeton was Janet's old love, the guy who had thrown her over before she married me. Luckily, I knew it too, so if the group was waiting for a dumb question from me, like "Who is Dick Templeton?" they were going to be disappointed.

You never know with good old friends, but the two

31

of us carried it off just fine. I ate another forkful of pasta, and Janet was casual when she asked,

"Really? How is Dick? You remember the name, don't you, Andy? I'm sure I told you about him."

I shrugged. "You've told me about so many old boyfriends, I just can't keep up. Which one was he?"

That defused the situation, and after that it was Marge Green who did the questioning. Janet didn't say another word, but I could tell she was listening hard.

"What's Dick doing in New York?" Marge asked.

"He's moving back from California," Hal said. "He's opening his own company in Connecticut to design small boats. Says he's already got a few good contracts."

"How many kids does he have?"

Hal shrugged. "Who knows? I don't even know if he's married."

Someone changed the subject after that, and small talk went on. Nothing fascinating was said, and I closed my eyes and dozed until Janet poked an elbow in my ribs. We left the Greens after that and walked home via the wooden boardwalk that roller-coastered over the dunes.

Back at our house, Janet asked, "Do you always have to fall asleep at parties? It's embarrassing."

"Darling, I'm tired, and I haven't seen you all week. Let's go to bed and see what happens next. What d'you say?"

Janet said nothing and got ready for bed. She took her makeup off, which took about ten minutes, and then her clothes. She then put on a nightgown and a sweater and got into bed beside me. I reached over and got a handful of clothes.

"Do you always have to wear so many clothes to bed?"

"I get cold. You know I have bursitis in one shoulder, and what if one of the girls wakes up during the night?"

However, with a sigh she took off her clothes. We embraced, groped each other. In a short time I rolled on top of her and came. She didn't. She put her clothes back on, moved over to her side of the bed and we both went to sleep. It was very different and a long time away from our first meeting at the beach.

The rest of the weekend was spent mostly with my kids, shopping at the market, taking them to the beach, preparing their meals, drinking more vodka-and-tonics.

One thing I did enjoy was chess. Hal Green likes chess as much as I do, and when I could send the kids off to play, I'd sneak in a game or two with Hal. I would have been happy to play chess all day, but Janet would get pissed and complain that I wasn't paying enough attention to the kids.

On Sunday night I ran into Hal on the boat going back. He took a small chess set with magnetic pieces out of his pocket, and we started to play. Janet wasn't around to complain.

"Janet seems a little down these days," Hal said, after the fourth move.

"Has she said anything to you or Marge?" I asked.

"Not exactly, but Marge says that Janet goes down to the marina whenever she can; you know she's crazy about sailing. Andy, why don't you buy her a Sailfish? They're not expensive, and she could handle it easily.

She used to handle a lot bigger boats when she was around with Dick.''

"Yeah, I know.''

"So why not buy her a small boat?''

I told Hal I'd think about it, and we went back to the chess board. We didn't finish our game before the boat docked. Hal had his car parked nearby, and he drove me home. I went up to our apartment, grateful to be alone, grateful for the quiet.

CHAPTER IV

Martine

New York is a wonderful place. There's always lots to do. Except on weekends. Weekends are when people stay home and catch cold, or go away, or buy loads of stuff in Bloomingdale's that they don't need, or stay in all day Sunday and read the *Times* and feel scruffy. That's a typical New York weekend, if you're a New Yorker. I've always envied the out-of-towners who come to New York, spend a weekend at the Plaza, eat out, go to the theater, and have a great time. That's exactly what I do when I'm in Boston, Chicago, or San Francisco for the weekend. That is not what I do in New York on weekends, because as Dee Dee says, "A weekend in New York is strictly amateur night." Which means that the restaurants are filled with groups of eight and ten from Paramus, New Jersey and you can never get a decent table, and the theaters are filled with nice people from Fontana, Wisconsin who giggle

35

if they hear a "shit" or a "fuck" said onstage, and have in-depth conversations during intermission, cawing and crying, "But what does it mean?"

I have my own weekend pattern, however, which works for me. I avoid the department stores after noon on Saturday, refuse dinner invitations for Saturday nights, and stay home on Sunday and read the *Times*. I may or may not answer the phone from Saturday morning until Monday morning.

Things I do on weekends:

I go to the Metropolitan Museum on Sunday as soon as it opens, and if the Lehman Collection is open I visit my favorite Lucas Cranach nude and wonder how a sixteenth-century painter and friend of Luther's could paint such elegantly slim and delightfully evil-looking women.

I go to the food shop at Bloomingdale's and buy Scotch smoked salmon, Boursault cheese, Black Forest ham, three kinds of bread, and a bagful of Famous Amos cookies. I eat a variety of cold appetizers all weekend, washed down with half bottles of a pretty good French champagne.

I work on weekends, because that's what free-lancers do, they work when they get the assignments and worry the rest of the time.

I buy a stack of books at Doubleday's and have an orgy of reading.

I watch all the old movies on TV, preferably Humphrey Bogart, and I have an orgy of TV watching.

I see my mother on weekends. We take a walk on Madison Avenue, looking at the shops and trying on clothes that neither one of us can possibly afford in the boutiques.

36

"I thought I'd die when you asked to see that Saint Laurent in red," my mother said.

"Why?"

"It was twenty-three hundred dollars."

"I wasn't going to buy it."

"I know that. But the way you act, the saleswoman believed that you might."

"You taught me everything I know, mom."

Things I don't do on weekends:

I avoid going out with men who think it would be great to take a walk though Central Park and look at all the people at Bethesda Fountain, and "maybe have a drink afterwards, and maybe go up to your place."

I avoid going out with men who think it would be great to take a drive into the country, and have dinner at a little Inn, little Auberge, little Japanese Garden. With all the great restaurants in New York, I don't see driving in bumper-to-bumper traffic to get to a restaurant with a bumper-to-bumper line.

I don't go to Chinese restaurants on Sundays. Sunday is the big family day for Chinese restaurants, and if you're not careful you can be hit by a flying eggroll thrown by a kid happy to be anywhere that isn't McDonald's.

I don't go to movies on Sunday. You wouldn't believe the lines.

As you can see, weekends are hibernation time for me, unless I'm out of town seeing the sights in some other city. And weekends are also when I have time. Lots of time to think. Maybe too much time.

I was happily married once. Davy and I had met in college, and we went through our junior and senior years hand-in-hand. Maybe it's the sort of romance that can only happen when you're eighteen, but it was a romance, warm, sweet and tender, and we married a few weeks after graduation. Three years later Davy was dead. The details are grim and have nothing to do with this story. I was in my early twenties when Davy died, but I knew I'd never remarry. Davy was too hard an act for any man to follow, and though I went out a lot and slept around a little, I never met anyone who interested me—not with the deep, no-holds-barred feeling I had known with Davy.

The fact that I didn't marry again and wasn't seriously interested in doing so was the despair of my parents. I was a beloved, only child, and my father spoke of that despair just a few hours before he died.

"What's going to happen to you?" he asked.

I expressed the selfishness of a grownup chid when I answered, "Don't worry, I'll be all right."

It was my mother with the courage born of her love for my father who was able to take his hand and say, "We're going to be all right. You'll get well, and the three of us will be just fine."

I knew that current psychological jargon advises telling the dying the absolute truth, but the hell with that. I remember that my mother's words had taken the fear of death from my father's face.

Now there was just my mother left to fret and worry about what was going to happen to me. My father had died in his fifties, but I never imagined the same thing would happen to my still young mother. And I reasoned that it didn't matter whom you loved, as long as you loved someone. I loved my mother, had my friends, my work, and I was content to drift along, not feeling too much about any man I went out with.

I enjoyed going out, but wake up with a man beside me every morning? I didn't want that. But! My brain flashed a picture of Andrew Lang. Maybe with someone like that it wouldn't be so bad. It might be nice to find Andrew Lang in my bed. He certainly had broad shoulders. Might be nice shoulders to lie on.

". . . Rest your head on my shoulders . . ."

How did that dumb song go?

And why was I thinking of him, anyway?

"It's delightful to be married . . . to be . . . to be . . . to be . . . to be married."

I had recently seen *The Great Ziegfeld* on the "Late Late Movie," and that was Louise Rainer's trilling song some scenes before her famous telephone farewell to Flo.

Well, never mind, maybe it was delightful to be married. Or maybe it wasn't. But there was no point in thinking of Andrew Lang. The man was spoken for and I had my rules, and the way he talked about his kids, so did he.

Oh, those Fire Island ladies, what they didn't know could fill a library. Or maybe they did know. That was Dee Dee's theory.

"They know, but they don't care. They got this guy, and he lays them, and they have a kid or two, and the poor guy is grateful forever and supports them forever. So what do they care if he's also laying someone else? It's probably a big relief to them."

"But—"

"What but? Listen, if you liked a guy, would you leave him alone in Fun City for a month or two, except for weekends?"

"No."

"So?"

That was Dee Dee's theory, and I can't say she was wrong. I don't know the answer to the question of who creates a summer bachelor, and I suppose Dee Dee's explanation is as good as any other.

I guess this is the time to tell you about Peregrine. What kind of name is that? It's the very English name of a very English writer, my friend Peregrine Marsh. To give you some idea of the kind of man Peregrine is, he is never, but never called Perry. He hates the practice of American nicknames; he doesn't think it's jolly, or fun, or even just a little amusing.

In my list of things I do and I don't do on weekends, Peregrine is on the *do* list. I do Peregrine, or maybe he does me, however you prefer to think of it.

Peregrine is always pointing out to me how very much we have in common.

Things we have in common according to Peregrine:

We are both free-lance writers.

We both work crazy hours, and are therefore free to go to the midnight *Rocky Horror Show* movie.

We both like to travel; and because we write books, we could live abroad. Together.

We laugh at the same things. (Well, some of the time.)

We love Chinese food, especially moo-shu pork.

We're both impatient with people who ask us if we write under our own names. (That means that while we both make good money, we're not famous, and who likes to be reminded of that?)

On weekends, Peregrine and I frequently do some hibernating together. Usually on Saturday nights we have dinner either at his apartment or mine, and whatever happens after that is okay with both of us.

Peregrine's good-looking, and everybody is impressed when I take him to a party. As Peregrine frequently reminds me, we are right for each other. We do the same work, like the same things, my friends like him, his friends like me.

So what is wrong? I'll tell you the truth. Here I am, twenty-nine, and I'm still expecting lights to flash when I make love. I still want to think that the earth can move. Hemingway did more to create sexual dissatisfaction than he knew.

When I'm in bed with Peregrine and he politely asks me, "Was it all right?" I just as politely say, "Yes, it was."

Only it wasn't. Not really.

Peregrine seems satisfied, but then, for all his good looks, he just isn't a very sexy man, and what's right for Peregrine is just not right for me. It's not bad as a sometime thing, but spend my life, or at least a lot of years with Peregrine? I don't think so.

This weekend Peregrine is away, exploring Washington, D.C. for one of those travel guides that takes you around the world dollar by dollar. I try to tell myself that I miss Peregrine, that the weekend in New York would be a lot more interesting if he were around. But I'm lying to myself. Peregrine isn't around. And I'm relieved.

CHAPTER V

Andy

Monday morning and I was back at the office. Jim came in, carrying his cup of black coffee.

"How'd you make out with Martine?" he asked, as he plopped down on my sofa. He was smiling as he asked. I knew he wanted to tell me how he had made out.

"How was she?" I asked.

Still grinning. "Kind of crazy. I can't figure her out. As soon as we got to her apartment she practically ripped her clothes off and mine too, which was great. In bed she was sort of frenzied, like some kind of athlete, the way she moved around. But after she came, she practically threw me out. She lit a cigarette and said, 'Don't you have to be somewhere?' But I'm not complaining. She gave good head. But what about you and Martine? She seemed to like you."

"Nothing happened," I said. "I took her home from

43

the restaurant. She lives in one of the boxes on the East Side. In front of the doormen—she's got two, not one—she shook my hand, thanked me for dinner, and said goodnight.''

"You going to see her again?''

"I don't know. I didn't ask her. Maybe.''

Jim left. His parting words were, "Better luck next time.'' He meant the better man had won. Again.

I suddenly realized I had thought about Martine over the weekend. I was on my way to a meeting, so I dropped it from my mind. But after lunching with the client, I got out the phone book, looked up Martine Lukas, and there she was. What the hell? I had nothing better to do. I dialed her number.

"Hi, this is Andy Lang.''

"Oh . . . hello.'' Friendly, but hesitant.

"Have a good weekend?''

"So-so. How about you?''

"Not bad, went to Fire Island. The weather was nice.''

"How are your kids?''

Why did she always have to ask about my kids? I started to talk fast. "I was wondering if you'd like to come with me to the Metropolitan? I mean the museum. It's open late on Tuesday, and I thought we could amble around the Lehman Collection. Get a chance to see how the rich folks spend their money. After, we could have dinner.''

She didn't answer right away. But finally she said okay, and asked what time we would meet.

I offered to pick her up at her apartment, but she gave me this story about her place being a mess, so I

44

suggested we meet at the seal pond of the Central Park Zoo.

"The seals. All right. I'll meet you there at five-thirty," and she hung up.

I got there before she did. As I entered the park, I passed a balloon vender, and I bought a large red balloon and waited for her at the seal pond holding the balloon string.

She saw me from a distance holding the balloon and she started running toward me.

"You got me a balloon?" She pulled it from my hand. "I love balloons. I must have told you."

With one hand she took the balloon and put her other hand in my arm. I made a muscle (I wonder if she felt it). Boy, was I conscious of that warm hand through my jacket.

We watched the seals for a while, then got a cab and went to the museum. As we walked through the museum she kept looking up at the balloon and saying how pretty it was, as it swayed back and forth on the string.

I think she spent more time looking at the balloon than the paintings. I know we kept getting a lot of stares from people. We enjoyed the attention. There was a couple with a small chid who suddenly cried out to her parents, "I want a balloon!" They looked embarrassed, then appealingly at us.

Martine said, "I'm an only child. This balloon is mine and I'm not sharing it."

After debating between eating at the museum or a new French restaurant on Eighty-sixth Street, we decided on the French restaurant, Chez Pascal.

We had no trouble getting a table even though we

didn't have reservations. It wasn't "in" yet, apparently. I think "in" restaurants won't let you in without a reservation even if they have tables. The waiter brought over the menus. Martine had a brief discussion with him in French about some of the items on the menu, and made her selection. Since she obviously knew more about the food than I did, I asked her to order for me, too. I chose the wine.

The food came. She had ordered quenelles de brochet with Nantua sauce for both of us. It tasted fine to me. A French version of my mother's gefilte fish. Only at home we put horseradish sauce on it, while this was a lot more delicate.

"This is good, isn't it?" I said.

She shook her head slightly. "It's not sauce Nantua. Quenelles should have sauce Nantua. I make it on special occasions but it's a lot of work."

"You mean you can really make this dish?"

"Sure."

"How?"

"Well, in the immortal words of my aunt who is a great cook, I wash my hands, put on my apron, and make it."

"I'd love to taste it. When can I come for dinner?"

"I don't know. Sometime."

"When?"

I kept pressing her. Hell, it wasn't the dinner I was thinking of, not entirely. I just kept wondering and hoping about what would happen if the two of us were someplace alone.

"When?" I asked again.

No soap. The best I could do was an invitation for lunch at Martine's club. Was she kidding? Okay, if

46

she wanted to put me off, why shouldn't I let her pay for lunch? We made a date for the following Friday.

We left the restaurant, Martine clutching the balloon in one hand, and practically cooing to it. Her other hand held my arm. It was a warm night, so she suggested we walk.

When we arrived at her apartment house I got the same deal as I had the time before.

"Do you mind if I say goodnight now?" she said in front of her apartment building. "I've got work that's due tomorrow."

"You're going to work at this time of night?"

"I work mostly at night. When you called I had just finished breakfast. That's what free-lance writers do. We don't work nine to five like you businessmen."

"Can't I come up for a quick cup of coffee?"

"Not even a cup of coffee."

"Okay, then, I'll see you for lunch Friday. Right?"

"Right."

She stood on her toes, reached over and kissed me lightly on the cheek and went into the house quickly, almost on tiptoes, still holding the balloon. I watched her, hoping she'd turn around and change her mind. She didn't.

I went home, undressed, got into bed, picked up a book, and started to read. But thoughts about Martine kept crowding in. I couldn't concentrate on the book. It was disturbing. I kept thinking about her hair. Her childlike ingenuousness that was so funny and disarming. Her hand holding my arm.

I turned out the light and tried to go to sleep. No good. It wouldn't work. I was getting angry. I've had affairs before. Sexually very exciting, but brief. I didn't

47

want to get involved. Why did I keep thinking about her? I just wanted to get laid. Come on, you're a married man. It's not a bad marriage compared to other marriages. And you've got two kids you're crazy about and they're crazy about you. Stop thinking about her. She's a piece of ass. That's all. Maybe you'll make it with her. Maybe you won't. But don't get involved. Don't look for trouble. Maybe it would be better if you canceled the lunch date. Maybe. Oh, what the hell. We'll see.

I turned on the Late Show. They had a Bogart movie. One of the forgettable ones. But its inanity and torturous plot were distracting and boring enough to put me finally to sleep.

CHAPTER VI

Martine

If it wasn't for that not-so-terrible-but-not-so-great weekend, I probably wouldn't have agreed to see that married-man-with-two-children Andrew Lang when he called me on Monday.

Look, I know why he called. I have no illusions about these guys who are on the loose for the summer. But he called at a moment when I was pretty disgusted with what was available. And then, as my friend Dee Dee says, "You have to eat, don't you? So why not let someone else pick up the check?" That's Dee Dee, nothing if not practical.

And I still might have said no, if he hadn't asked me to go with him to the Metropolitan Museum before dinner. I absolutely love the Metropolitan on Tuesday nights. I like to walk around those marble halls and pretend that I live there.

Now that the Lehmans have so kindly added their

collection and insisted that it be housed in a building that copies rooms in the old family townhouse, it's even easier for me to fantasize about living in the museum.

Of course, Andy wanted to pick me up at my apartment, and of course I said no. We finally decided to meet at the seal pond in Central Park. And again, he struck a chord. I love seals. I love the way they bark and flap their flippers, and I would never, but never, buy a seal coat, even though I could afford one.

And what I haven't told anyone: Davy and I spent many an afternoon while we were in college visiting the seals. Davy was proud of the way he could imitate a seal's bark. He did it so well the seals would swim over to the side of the pool and look up at him hopefully.

"There you are," Davy would say, pleased that he had arranged to have the seals swimming at my feet. "There you are."

Don't be ridiculous, I told myself as I took the Fifth Avenue bus to Fifty-ninth Street and Central Park. The guy is on the make, and you can't go to bed with him because of seals or a visit to the Metropolitan. Listen, you've been offered more than that: weekends in Jamaica, for example, and one high roller even mentioned a week in Paris.

That was one way of looking at it. Another way was to take things and men the way Dee Dee took them. What was wrong with a casual roll in the hay? Nothing, except that try as I might, I've never been the casual type.

I decided that I was just giving too much thought to the whole thing. As Dee Dee said, I had to eat, and someone else might as well pick up the check. After dinner I'd say goodnight, and that would be that.

I kind of dragged my feet walking into the park. Why was I bothering with this guy? Him and his talk about his two beautiful kids. I was sure they were beautiful. Far more beautiful in his eyes than I could ever be. I was feeling kind of melancholy when I passed the cage with the two aoudads, and then seeing the dumb-looking camel didn't make me feel any better. Wasn't it time that I stopped seeing people who could never mean anything to me? Maybe Peregrine wasn't such a bad bet after all. At least he didn't go on about his beautiful children.

My steps really slowed as I walked towards the seal pond.

That familiar feeling of guilt was with me. I was alive, and Davy wasn't. Davy had been dead six years, but I still remembered the way it was. Can you believe I felt guiltier about going to see the seals than I had about sleeping with other men after Davy died?

Maybe Andy wouldn't be there, and then I could say he was late and I just didn't feel like waiting. Or maybe even if he was there I would just explain that something came up, a rush assignment, and that I just had come to say I couldn't have dinner with him. Or maybe I would just turn around and go back home. He wouldn't wait forever, and then he'd have a free evening to go home and think some more about his beautiful kids.

But then I saw him standing there. Saw him before he saw me. Saw dark hair that curled slightly and needed a bit of a haircut. Something about that hair. It made him seem boyish and kind of vulnerable. And then I saw that he was holding onto something. It was wrapped around his fist, actually. A string attached to a red balloon that floated and bobbed above his head. There was something so damn *hopeful* about that balloon. Something so young. Something that a high-school boy in Canton, Ohio might have gotten for his girl at the county fair.

I didn't mean to do it. I had really thought I was going to turn back. But instead I was running, running towards him.

"A balloon," I said, reaching for the string, completely forgetting to say hello. "You got me a balloon."

He handed me the balloon, and we walked and talked and finally took a taxi to the Metropolitan Museum where we walked and talked some more. I forgot about Davy. I forgot about Andy's wife, and I even forgot about his beautiful children. Except I was reminded, just a little, when a kid in the museum wanted me to give her my balloon.

I held on to the balloon more tightly, and I thought kids want everything, don't they? Well, maybe they're entitled. But I'm a child, too. And an only child at that.

Andrew Lang laughed at me for not giving my balloon to that other child at the museum, but it wasn't a bad laugh. Peregrine would have said, "How can you be so silly." But then Peregrine wouldn't have bought me a balloon in the first place.

I expected Andrew to take me to a nice-but-cheap hamburger place after the museum. I know summer bachelors; they're great for wanting something, if not for nothing, then not for too much. But he surprised

52

me again by suggesting Chez Pascal, which is one of the in and expensive French restaurants in New York.

Pascal's is pleased to have a rustic setting. Oak beams, oak floors, oak tables, decorated ceramic wall tiles. Just like the French countryside, except that if they charged like that in the French countryside, they'd have another French revolution on their hands. Their prices were enough to make me gasp, and I guess it was because of that that I gave the captain a small argument about the sauce that decorated the pike quenelles.

"For that price they should serve a genuine sauce Nantua," I told Andy, "crushed lobster shells and all."

A minute later I was sorry I had said it, because he kept making obvious hints about my cooking dinner for him at my place. Part of it was my fault, of course, for letting him know that my mother came from France and that I knew more than just a little about food.

"Someday," I said, with what I hoped he would take for a Gallic shrug that meant maybe never.

"When?" he persisted.

I fell back on the hearty pose of a businesswoman. "How about lunch instead? At my club?"

I was halfway joking. Lunch at the club. Too British, too phony. I did use the club for client lunches. But he was no client, though we had talked for half a second about the possibilities of my doing some freelance advertising copy for him.

He surprised me. "Terrific! When?"

Oh, for heaven's sake! But I had invited him, and so I made a date. Well, why not? I suppose I owed him something for the expensive dinner, and the only thanks he was going to get from me was lunch at my club. Better for me than having to say thank you in bed. Only I couldn't understand his accepting at all. We dawdled a little longer over café filtre and cassis sherbet that was really boysenberry, and then I let him take me home. Home meaning the entrance of my apartment building. I shut my ears to hints about nightcaps or another cup of coffee, but when I shifted my red balloon from my right hand to my left I realized how silly I was being.

This guy was no Jack the Ripper. I could have invited him up. Men don't buy girls balloons if they're planning to rape them. It just didn't fit. But it was too late for second thoughts, so I just said, "Goodnight, thanks for dinner, see you Friday at the club," and I rushed in through the front door as though I were sixteen and not a widder lady of twenty-nine.

After I let myself into my apartment, I let the balloon float to the ceiling. The helium was already dribbling away, and the balloon balanced somewhere between ceiling and floor.

"Nothing lasts," I reminded myself as I had been reminding myself for six years.

By Friday I decided to stop all this nonsense. Enough silliness unto the day. I would take him to lunch, he would go off to Fire Island for the weekend, and then that would be finally and truly that. Why drag this never-can-be thing on?

By Friday I was wishing I could call the whole stupid lunch off. Why didn't I? I just figured it would be easier to say goodbye after we'd met one more time. He took me to dinner, I'd take him to lunch. All was even and balanced, and that would be that.

I didn't have the guts to tell Dee Dee that I was taking Andrew Lang to lunch at my club. She takes a

54

very dim view of women picking up checks. I tell her that's old fashioned thinking.

"That's me," Dee Dee says, "I'm a very old-fashioned girl."

I got to the club before he did. That's my curse; I'm prompt. Talk about old-fashioned. I never get to make the grand entrance, because I'm never late.

Not that he was late. He was on time, and I did my bit about greeting him in the club lounge. Why was I acting so pleased to see him? Come on, let's get this over with.

Mr. Holloway, the club's maitre d', knew that I used the club for business entertaining, and he was his usual solicitous self. Did I want a table in the grill or the main dining room? I turned to Andrew Lang, and I could see that he was impressed. Like a little boy. Was he going to say, "Oh, wow"?

I knew what it was, of course. Not too many women use a university club for entertaining; just as not too many women pick up checks, even at business lunches. Liberation or not, they still have trouble handling it. As one smart woman financial writer once told me, "I don't know how to figure out the tip."

My heart sank. It was that boyish bit all over again. Not in a phony way, either. And I'm just child enough to enjoy other adults who never grew up.

Stop being so Peter Pan. This guy is plenty grown up. He even has two children to prove it.

He started again about having dinner at my house. A mean little streak in me wanted to say, "Sure, how about tomorrow, Saturday night?" Knowing damn well he would be in Fire Island with his loved ones.

He kept it up, and looking at him across the table,

looking at those shoulders, the dark, wavy hair, I was having a hard time remembering just why it was I had decided not to see him again.

Finally I said, "Okay. Wednesday. How about Wednesday?"

"No," he said. "How about Monday?"

My heart started to pound. What was the rush? By Wednesday I could think up some good excuses to put him off. If it was Wednesday I could call him Tuesday and cancel.

"Monday," said the Red Balloon Buyer. "Monday, please."

"Okay, Monday," said the Nut Of The World.

We left the club and got into the elevator that would take us to the street. The sane, sensible street where the hot sun would surely bring me to my senses. I must talk to the manager of the club. I think the lights are too dim in there; they create false moods.

We were out on the street. I blinked in the sun and took a deep breath of lung-searing, disgusting New York July air. There, that was more like it. Cleared the thought passages.

"Monday," he said.

"Yes," I repeated, "Monday."

CHAPTER VII

Andy

We met at Martine's club on Friday. I was expecting a whole building like the Harvard Club, or the Princeton Club. Instead the NYU Club was on the third floor of the Town Hall building. I got out of the elevator, passed the cigarette stand and check room, and entered a large lounge filled with overstuffed chairs and sofas flanked by cocktail tables with a few magazines tossed around.

Martine was sitting on one of the sofas facing the entrance, reading a magazine. I was only about five minutes late, but she was there. Well, why not? This whole thing was her idea. But I was very pleased to see her.

As soon as she saw me coming towards her, she put down her magazine, stood up, and greeted me by extending her hand. She looked fine, except that I thought her dress was terrible. It was loose, like a smock. I thought only sloppy painters wore smocks. But what was even worse, it had a large flounce at the bottom. I hate flounces. The hell with her dress. I concentrated instead on the lovely, dark hair framing her face.

Martine signaled to a waitress who came right over and she ordered our drinks in the lounge.

"White wine for me," she said, "and a very dry vodka martini on the rocks with a twist."

She remembered what I drank. The drinks came, and they were generous. As we sat and sipped the maitre'd came downstairs from the restaurant, menus under his arm.

He approached Martine, smiling broadly. "Hello, Mrs. Lukas. Your table is ready whenever you want it. If you're in a hurry you can order now."

Martine turned to me. "Are you in a hurry?"

"Not me. I'd like to finish my drink and have another one upstairs before lunch, if that's okay with you."

The maitre d' smiled approval and left with his menus.

We went upstairs a few minutes later and I saw that the dining room was spacious and pleasant. It had no special character or motif, no university signs or banners. It was just a large, comfortable room, tables not too close together, with captain's chairs. The menu matched it. It was plain, wholesome American food, steaks, chops, hamburgers, salads. The food wouldn't distract us from our conversation. We had another drink and she wrote on an order form, handing it to the waitress. Everybody who worked at the restaurant seemed to know her. They all smiled when she passed and welcomed her. I was impressed.

Over lunch I learned that Martine was a widow. I wondered, was she still carrying a torch? But then she told me it had been six years. Not even the best of men are remembered that long. Martine didn't say too much about him, and I was secretly pleased that she didn't have any children. I love kids as long as they're mine, but I've never been able to get interested in anyone else's.

Martine didn't seem to be that way, however. She kept bringing up my family, especially my children, but I was in no mood to talk about them. All I wanted to do was to talk about her, think about her, touch her hair, speculate on what she looked like under that silly dress, and a few other things that had nothing to do with my children.

"This is a lovely lunch," I said, "but it's not the kind of food I expected. When are you inviting me to dinner? Failing that, would you have dinner with me next week? Those are your two choices."

"All right, dinner at my house. How about Wednesday?"

"How about Monday?"

She laughed and agreed. Monday at six.

I almost asked for the check when I remembered that in private clubs, only the members can pay and she had already signed for the check when she ordered the lunch. It was all very discreet and elegant.

We parted and I went back to the office to straighten my desk and catch the train to Fire Island, the kids, the wife.

The ferry ride was not too pleasant. My thought kept bouncing like a ping-pong ball back and forth between Martine and my family. In truth, I really didn't want to see my family. I wanted to be with Martine. I wanted to touch her, go to bed with her. I wondered what would she be like in bed. What did she look like without clothes? She kept crowding out all other thoughts. I would force myself to think about the kids, and Janet. How was I going to behave over the weekend? Drink a lot, that would help pass the time. Sleep a lot, that's even better. See a lot of people. Get distracted.

The boat docked with the usual number of kids shouting "Daddy." My kids were there, too, with my wife. She was wearing one of those loose fitting mid-length shifts designed to hide a woman's shape or size. Why do women do things like that? My wife had a nice figure. Why did she always seem to hide or abuse her appearance? Was it just to stay in fashion? Or did she dress that way because she knew I didn't like it? I decided not to think about Martine and to try to enjoy my wife and kids. I made up my mind I was going to be specially attentive.

"Have you planned anything for dinner tonight?" I asked Janet.

"I thought we'd have hamburgers."

"Let me do dinner tonight," I said. "And how about going out to dinner tomorrow night? You've been cooking all week."

She looked surprised but pleased, and said "But I've invited Hal and Marge Green for dinner tomorrow."

"No problem. We'll take them to dinner, too. I feel rich today. Besides, I don't want you working all day, preparing dinner. Let's spend some time together."

We got back to the house and I cooked the dinner. I made Hamburger Basquaise. That's fancy hamburger made with tomatoes, onions, and a few spices. I was once a pretty good cook, having learned as a bachelor in order to induce women to come to my apartment. It was cheaper than taking dates to restaurants, and once they were in the apartment it seemed easier to get them into bed. As a matter of fact, that's how I started my affair with Janet, which ended in our marriage. I think the affair was more fun.

We had dinner and I put the kids to bed. We had a few drinks. I told Janet about the office events of the week. She told me about her exercise class and some of the Fire Island gossip, and we went to bed.

We made love. I was particularly avid. I wanted to be good, and she was surprised by my extra attention and seemed to respond a little too, and we finally went to sleep.

I didn't know why I was so attentive to my wife that weekend. I know Martine kept appearing in my mind, and every time she did I would try to do or say something pleasing to Janet. I would find myself fantasizing about the forthcoming dinner with Martine. What would it be like? I would imagine a beautiful scene, candlelight, wine, and finally sex. I was undressing her. She was beautiful. Then I would snap back and pay attention to Janet and my kids.

So help me, I even invented different scenarios in my fantasies. One, she phones me Monday morning and calls it off. She tells me she's going to California for an indefinite period. Two, the dinner is rotten. She's a shrew, complains all through dinner. I end up in a wrestling match with her, I get her undressed and find she wears a padded bra and she's bony all over. I even put pimples on her skin.

It didn't help much. She kept reappearing. But I managed to get through the weekend in a way that pleased Janet and made me feel less guilty. Yet on the trip back to the city, I let Martine consume all my thoughts. As soon as I arrived at my apartment I made myself a martini and called Martine. She was home. We talked about our weekends. Hers was all right. Mine was all right. How are your kids? All right. What did you do? Blah, blah, blah. I didn't really say what I was thinking. I enjoyed hearing her voice while I lay on my bed sipping my martini. We must have talked for over a half hour about nothing important. The dinner for Monday evening was on.

CHAPTER VIII

Andy

When I was a boy growing up, a glamorous, un-married aunt of mine once confided to me that there's hardly a woman alive who can resist a man who brings flowers. So when I arrived at Martine's house that Monday for dinner I was carrying a large box with long-stemmed, deep red roses. Actually, I can't resist flowers either, but I guess it's considered sissy to give a man flowers, so if I want flowers, I have to buy them for myself.

When Martine opened the door and saw the box under my arm, her eyes opened wide and she didn't even wait for me to offer them to her.

"For me? I love flowers," and she practically pulled the box out of my arm. My aunt was right.

"May I come in?"

She looked up at me, a little embarrassed, and laughed. "Of course." She reached up and gave me a light kiss, but this time on the lips, took my arm, and ushered me into the apartment. "Make yourself comfortable. I'll put these flowers in a vase and I'll be right out," and she disappeared into another room.

I liked what she was wearing this time. It was a long dress with a low scoop neck showing the slightest cleavage, and tucked in at the waist. I finally saw she had a woman's shape. I didn't sit down at first. I just strolled around the living room. It was warm and luxurious. Full curtains against a wall, carpeting covering the floors. No chairs, just couches covered in brilliantly hued Thaibok silk. I guess if you don't have kids you can have silk sofas. My eyes were drawn to a corner of the room where I saw an oversized chaise covered in red velvet. It said lie down. I headed for it immediately. I guess I'm like the French. I think everything is better viewed from a reclining position.

I sat down on the edge tentatively. There was a tea-cart next to the chaise with plates of hors d'oeuvres. They were beautifully laid out. Pâté with crackers, sliced raw vegetables with a bowl of sauce next to it. In the midst of this elegant and luxurious apartment, Bemelmans drawings dotted the walls, those wonderful childlike illustrations of Madeleine and his other characters. They said to me, "Don't take this room too seriously."

"Martinis, right?" She came into the room carrying a tray with a pitcher and two glasses with ice in them. "I'll join you."

She sat down next to me on the chaise.

"Sit back, that's what the chaise is for," she said as she poured the drinks into the glasses. "Can I fix you a plate of hors d'oeuvres? There's a pâté I made, and try the crudités with the sauce.''

She made up a plate for me and left the room for a minute to return with the flowers in a vase. She was stroking the petals. ''They're so soft, so velvety.'' She held them up to her face and stroked her face with the petals. She finally put the vase down and sat down on the edge of the chaise where I was reclining, and gave her attention to me.

She looked marvelous. Her long hair framed her oval face, and she was radiant as she smiled and kept chattering. I didn't hear a word she was saying. I was thinking her hair and face would be a lot nicer to touch than the petals on the roses. A lot softer, too. I kept sipping my drink until finally I could stand it no longer. I sat up, bringing my face closer to hers, reached out and put my hand out and started stroking her hair. She gave a little shiver. She didn't stop me, but she stopped chattering. My hand went down and I stroked her face with my fingertips. I was right, softer than rose petals. I leaned closer, pulled her face towards me with my hand, and kissed her on the lips. What happened after that still seems like a dream to me.

I remember all the symbols and clichés used in the movies to indicate rising passion and the sex act. And I'm talking about the movies made before they had X-ratings. There was the bit with the stallion rearing and whinnying, and then there was that other scene, where the fire in the fireplace suddenly flames up. I think if those symbols were used for what happened to me that night, the rearing stallion would end up walking on his hind legs like a pipe, and the fire would consume half the lumber in Canada.

It all seemed so natural the way she seemed to come to me. The light kiss turned into a deep, searching one as our mouths covered each other's. My hand on her head turned into two hands and arms around her body, and I was enveloping her.

I began to feel enveloped too, as if a cocoon were growing around me, caused by her hands touching me, the warmth of her embrace. She seemed to melt into me.

I don't know how I did it, but I found myself carrying her, so help me. I picked her up in my arms, and brought her into the bedroom. Our mouths never parted.

Somehow we found ourselves without clothes. I don't remember undressing, but I realized that not only didn't she wear falsies, she didn't wear a bra. Her body was smooth and soft like her face, and wonderfully curved.

She was beautiful. I don't remember exactly what happened next. You can't reconstruct sentences in your mind, or memories of pleasure or pain. But I do remember we touched and kissed and there were sounds that weren't sounds or words; they seemed to come from the body, not just the mouth.

Everything I did seemed to please her. I felt myself growing. All of me. I felt strong, tender, generous, commanding, protective, pleasing. There wasn't a part of her body I didn't make love to. And everywhere she touched me was an electrical event. When she leaned over to kiss me her falling hair seemed to be kissing me, too. We became so intertwined, it felt as if we were really one.

I don't remember coming. I know we both must

have, several times. But we would stop once in a while and sit up in bed and continue touching each other. Or she would put her head against my shoulder and chest and her hands would play with the hair on my chest. I would have my arm around her and stroke her neck and back. Then we would make love again. Coming would be a sort of signal to rest awhile. Nothing more. It wasn't a high point or a climax. It wasn't the greatest sensation, because the whole experience was so great that there could be no higher or lower point.

It was wonderful and the biggest surprise of my life. I'd made love to other women and enjoyed it most of the time. But this was different. Even to this day I don't understand exactly what happened, why I felt the way I did. Martine and I had other sexual experiences after that, marvelous ones, but not like that first time. We finally did stop.

"You must be hungry."

"I'm famished," and I reached for her again.

"No, I mean real food, the dinner I cooked for tonight."

"Okay, but can I help?"

"No, stay where you are. I'll be right back."

She got out of bed, put on a dressing gown and left the room. I smoked a cigarette. She came back soon wheeling a cart with dishes and napkins and everything else for dinner. "We'll eat here. Is that all right?"

We had dinner in the bedroom, complete with a veal dish in a cream-and-brandy sauce, an excellent white wine, chilled, fresh fruit for dessert and even brandy. But even while we ate we would reach out and touch each other.

After dinner she wheeled the tray and the dishes out

of the room and came back to bed. We lay next to each other and then made love again. It was the same as before, only a little lower, more languid, sleepy. We finally did go to sleep wrapped up in each other.

I woke with a start. It was still dark. I looked at my watch. It was five-thirty in the morning. Martine was still asleep. Thank God my wife was in Fire Island. But what if she'd called? What if she'd been trying to reach me? I'd better get home as fast as I could. I got out of bed and started dressing. Martine woke and saw me dressing. She asked me what time it was. When I told her, she sat up and offered to make me coffee. I told her not to bother, to stay in bed.

She watched me as I dressed hurriedly. When I was finished I leaned over to kiss her. She then said, "I'll see you to the door." She put on a robe. She put her arms around me, asked me to hug her, and told me to be careful on the way home.

When I left the building and emerged into the street I saw slight signs of dawn, but there was almost no movement in the street except for a passing truck or a hurrying cab.

Normally I didn't worry about receiving any late-night calls from Janet. I had never gotten one in the past. And she was such a heavy sleeper that only the howling of one of the kids or the outbreak of war with guns blazing and bombs bursting could wake her in the middle of the night. And since the kids were healthy and I didn't hear any bombs, I didn't panic, but I did worry some.

I got a cab quickly and was home in minutes. I checked the answering machine and there were no calls. Nothing had happened. I took a deep breath and let it out slowly. I got out of my clothes, and went to the bathroom and showered. I left the door open in case the phone did ring.

Afterward, I made coffee, and as I drank it I thought about Martine and the night before. Martine was something special.

CHAPTER IX

Martine

Just what I had been afraid of, he was good to lie against. Damn those shoulders. And I liked putting my head against his chest which was even broader without clothes than it had seemed all tucked into a suit. I kept trying to tell myself that I was making love to a married man, but the married part kept eluding me, and all I kept thinking about was the man. Andy Lang. Some man.

The guilt flooded me after he left. Davy, what am I doing to you? It wasn't sleeping with another man that made me feel so guilty, I had done that before. It was the caring. During the years since Davy's death I had worked it out in my head that it was all right sleeping with someone I didn't care about. The bad part, the betrayal, would be the caring. It had never come up before. Not even with Peregrine, whom I was closer to than any other man I knew.

You're entitled to your life . . . that's what my mother said. That's what my father had said. That's what my friends thought, without saying. But I didn't feel that way. I still owed Davy.

CHAPTER X

Andy

The next few weeks were a mixture of heaven and hell for me. There I was, a happily married man with two perfect children—and a mistress. But no ordinary mistress. I was falling in love. I was constantly thinking about her, not just the passion of the sex but her geisha-like qualities, the way she would cater to me, serve me, give me things. Like the time I went to her apartment after work and she had prepared dinner for us. It was the usual splendid meal. Course after course, each more delicious than the last, served effortlessly. Each would appear as if by magic, our conversation never losing a beat, the empty dishes disappearing as if by magic. I offered to help clear the table but Martine wouldn't let me.

Comparisons were inevitable. Janet was a good cook, too. If she prepared an elaborate meal, however, I knew all about all the work that had gone into it. From the moment I would arrive home I would be told how arduous Janet's day had been, the elaborate shopping, her triumph at the supermarket, her battle with the butcher, and how tired and worn out she was from preparing the meal while the children were underfoot. She expected me to help set and help clear the table and do the dishes. I kept saying to myself this kind of comparison was unfair, Martine had no kids and no husband to take care of.

Yet the comparisons would keep coming and Janet always lost no matter how reasonable and logical I tried to be. It was as though my head were divided into a tennis court with Martine on one side and Janet on the other. I was the ball or the referee. I couldn't even make up my mind as to the role I played.

The dinner was over. We had had fresh vegetables in a mayonnaise-type sauce, a rack of lamb the likes of which I had never tasted, and salad. We were having some cheese and fruit when Martine announced, "I have a special dessert for you," and left for the kitchen.

I expected a flaming crêpe, or a soufflé, or a mousse, a classic dessert that would go with this splendid meal. Instead Martine returned to the dining room pushing the serving cart before her. On it were two large, fluted dishes filled with ice cream, a small bowl over a warmer filled with hot fudge sauce and a large bowl overflowing with whipped cream.

"I made some fresh whipped cream, the ice cream is chocolate, and if you look next to the sauce you'll find some freshly shelled walnuts. The fudge is hot, help yourself."

Chocolate hot fudge sundae with nuts. If you think this isn't something very special, you're missing the best that American culture has to offer. A week earlier I had told Martine about my job at a soda fountain when I was a teenager. As an employee I could eat whatever I wanted before I left work. In the early days of my job I would make myself the most grandiose concoctions with everything the fountain had in stock. I would take the biggest dish we had, fill it with many different scoops of ice cream and pour every sauce and garnish over it: syrups, fruits, nuts, marshmallow, and whipped cream. Whatever we sold, I would try to eat in one sitting. I would stand in front of this mountain of goo—I couldn't sit because the concoction was too high—and slowly consume it, much to the amusement of my fellow workers and the proprietor who enjoyed my enthusiasm for ice cream and my gargantuan appetite.

After working at the soda fountain for a few weeks my ice cream fantasies became more realistic, and my nightly portion became more selective. Finally, through trial and error, I narrowed it down to a favorite, chocolate ice cream, hot fudge sauce, and nuts. I would have that sundae almost every night, never getting tired of it.

Now I was a grownup, I ate and drank what grownups eat and drink: vintage wines, martinis, soufflés, Sauce périgueux, things like that. No more childish things.

Martine remembered my story. Everything I told her she remembered. So she had surprised me with a sundae. That's what I mean by her geisha-like qualities. She just kept on pleasing me, heaping pleasure on pleasure.

Yet all this caring and giving and tenderness and

75

love only served to make me feel more guilty. My well-ordered life was being disturbed. I was living the American dream: an attractive wife, two kids, a good job that paid well, and even better prospects. Martine's role as a mistress could be part of the dream, too. I could afford it. What I couldn't afford was falling in love with Martine, and that's what I seemed to be doing.

My feelings about her started affecting my job. I would think about her constantly, what happened the night before, what was going to happen the next time we saw each other. Imagine having sexual fantasies about someone you're having a sexual relationship with already. I would wonder what she was doing at that moment, and then I would call her. I would call her every day. As a result I began making mistakes. I turned in work late. I forgot appointments. It wasn't like me. My secretary, Brenda, was the first to comment on it.

Brenda is a cute little redhead who came to New York from a wealthy suburb of Philadelphia to make her fortune or find a husband, whichever came first. I liked her; she was good at her job and she was pretty. We would flirt, and I would threaten her with sexual mayhem because of her provocative behavior. She would retaliate with an exaggerated wiggle of her behind as she left my office. It was fun, and we both knew it wasn't serious. I made certain by never touching her.

One morning after depositing my second cup of coffee on my desk she said, "Andy, are you in some kind of trouble or is something bothering you?"

"Everything's fine. Why?"

"Well, people are complaining. The traffic department can't get okays from you. Your conference reports are going out late or not going out at all, and your mail is piling up. You're not returning phone calls, and I'm getting blamed because they think you're not getting your messages. Other than that, everything is okay."

Her speech shook me up. I had a reputation which I had worked hard to develop. I was always on top of everything and I was thorough. The people who worked for me often called me a pain in the ass because I demanded thoroughness from them, too. Their complaints didn't bother me because my clients liked the service I gave them and counted on it. That's why I was well-paid. Brenda's comments had to be taken seriously, and my reveries about Martine had to be checked.

Bart Mitchell, the president of my agency, took care of that. He called me into his office that afternoon to tell me the agency was being invited to solicit a coffee account, a big one, and would I work with him on preparing the new business presentation.

The added work and responsibility was welcome in more ways than one. I was pleased that Bart had picked me to coordinate the presentation. If we got the account it could mean bigger things for me and a lot more money. It also gave me a chance to focus my energies and interests. I would concentrate on what was important in my life: my career and my family. I would stop being so moony about Martine and put her in proper perspective—a casual romance that would end soon. I was glad that the demands of the agency didn't leave me much free time.

I was into the new presentation for only a couple of

days when I got a call from Joe Noyes. Joe and I had grown up together, gone to the same university, and we were both in advertising—Joe as a copywriter, me on the account side. Until Janet and I had married, I had always considered Joe one of my closest friends, but over the last few years we hardly saw each other. We kept up with what was happening to the other through the little squibs in *Ad Age,* and we still had lunch once a year, but that was about it. At one time I was hurt at the way Joe acted. He had refused so many invitations to my house that I had stopped inviting him. But then I figured the hell with it. We probably didn't have very much in common any more. People drift apart. But when Joe called, I was happy to hear from him, and once we started talking it was as though we had seen each other just yesterday—not almost eight months before.

"Andy," Joe said, "any chance that you're free for lunch today?"

I had a lot of work to do and I had planned to eat at my desk, but my curiosity and former affection made me say, "Sure. Where and what time?"

We met at a restaurant near my office which was more famous for their drinks than their food, and when I arrived Joe was finishing a vodka-rocks, and he quickly ordered another. I saw he had put on weight—probably the vodka.

Our hellos were warm, and I said, "It's great to see you, Joe, I've been reading your articles in *Ad Age,* and it always says at the bottom of the page that you're a consultant. So how's the consulting business?"

"You know the lingo—consulting is another term

for out of work. I've been free-lancing for a bunch of agencies, and you know what that's like, too."

"I've been there. You're looking for a job."

"Yup, that's the sum and substance of it. I hear good things are happening at your shop, Andy, and I was hoping there might be something there for me."

"Let me ask around," I said. "I'll talk to the creative director."

"I'd appreciate it," Joe said.

With that out of the way we ordered more drinks and some food. As usual, it was good seeing Joe. We told jokes, shared gossip about people in our business. It was like old times. As a matter of fact, it was so much like old times that I had to ask the question that I had kept bottled up for years.

"Joe, how come we hardly see each other? We were good friends, or I thought we were, and then it ended. Look, I'm glad you called, even though it was for business reasons, but I'd still like to know what happened? Why did we lose touch?"

Joe hadn't looked uncomfortable when he had told me he was looking for a job, but he looked uncomfortable now.

"Hey, these things happen."

"Don't bullshit me, Joe."

"Andy, when a guy gets married, his single friends often disappear. Many wives don't like their husbands' single friends."

"You talking about Janet? Janet never said a word."

"She didn't have to. Look, I don't think we should go into this."

"No, come on. I want to know what happened."

"Nothing *happened*. Not like you mean. It's just that

I never felt comfortable at your house. If I flicked an ash into an ashtray, Janet was there cleaning it up. If I asked you for another drink, well, I could see the way she looked at me.

"Look, Andy, Janet's a great girl, great for you, but she didn't approve of me. Not what I did. Not the way I lived. I always got the feeling she was afraid I was going to lead you astray. I just figured it was best if I made myself scarce."

"I wish you had told me this before."

"What difference would it have made? Listen, forget it. Tell me about what's going on in your life. Any more kids?"

"No. Just the two."

"And how about the piano, you still got that big upright? Big Bertha we called it, right? You played the best jazz piano I ever heard. You've probably traded Big Bertha for a Bosendorfer grand, right?"

"Wrong," I said. "We had to get rid of Big Bertha after Diane was born. You know New York apartments—never enough space. We needed the room for a chest. Besides, Janet wasn't crazy about my playing."

"Yeah, well, pianos do take up a lot of room." Joe took a final swallow of his coffee. "Listen, Andy, thanks for seeing me today. I appreciate it."

"Sure, Joe. I'll call you as soon as I talk to the creative director. This afternoon. Tomorrow at the latest."

"Thanks, Andy, and I hope what I said—"

"Forget it, Joe."

I could tell Joe to forget it, but I couldn't. It wasn't only Joe I no longer saw. I hardly saw any of my old friends any more. They were a lot more raffish than the West and East Side crews we were now friendly with. Joe was right. A lot of men lost their old friends once they got married.

Talking to Joe bought Martine back into my mind. I wondered what he would think about the Red Balloon Kid. I called Martine, and once I heard her voice I knew how very much I wanted to see her. We made a date for dinner that night even though I had planned not to see her for a while.

We went to Chinatown, where we discovered a new Chinese restaurant. There are always new Chinese restaurants to discover in Chinatown—the food ranges from terrible to wonderful. It was so good to be with Martine that I enjoyed everything. We went back to her apartment after dinner, and I spent most of the night there. I left at dawn, went back to my apartment to change clothes, and went to work.

There was no question in my mind any longer about Martine. I wasn't going to fight it any more. Let it roll all over me. I liked the feeling. I was hooked.

CHAPTER XI

Martine

Rationalization is what keeps me going, and this is how I explained *l'affaire Lang* to myself:

I was only a summertime thing.

By the end of summer I would be so bored with the old broad-shouldered balloon buyer that I would be happy to say goodbye—just as I had been happy to say goodbye to many another summertime thing—or is it fling?

And if July comes, can Labor Day be far behind?

But I guess I wasn't too convinced by my rationalizations, because I also decided I needed an insurance policy. Just what is an insurance policy when you're having an affair with a man you shouldn't be having an affair with? Another man, of course.

Andy spent his weekends in Fire Island, so I decided to accept an invitation to Southampton.

"You're going to Southampton?" Andy asked.

"You're going to Fire Island?" I asked right back.

We both knew what it meant. He'd get tucked into bed with his wife on Friday and Saturday nights. He couldn't exactly say he had a headache. And I would get tucked into bed with a new man in Southampton, because that's why people went away for weekends, and that's why my friends had invited me for this one.

Were Corey Eldon and Bonnie Lambert my friends? They thought so, and from time to time, so did I. Corey was an editor of a magazine for which I did a lot of work, and Bonnie was the blonde nut he had left his wife for. They had been inviting me constantly to spend a weekend in their rented cottage at the beach, and Corey was even beginning to make noises about my being too aloof and how he didn't like to work with aloof writers. That made me nervous. Corey was a mainstay of my income.

"It's not that I'm aloof," I said, "I work on weekends. That's how free-lance writers work. We don't take off weekends when there's an assignment."

"You can't work seven days a week. It's not good for you. Besides, I feel there's a strain showing in your work, Martine. I can see it. You'll work better when you're not so tired. You better spend this weekend with Bonnie and me and another friend of ours."

"What friend?" I had met some of Corey and Bonnie's friends, and they did nothing but make me nervous. They thought that sniffing coke was child's play and they didn't understand how anyone could survive without dropping acid from time to time.

"No one you know," Corey said. "Mike Malloy from Chicago. He's a TV writer and producer. Give

84

it a chance, Martine. You might like this one for a change."

"I'll come out by train Saturday morning. Do you know the schedule?"

"Why don't you come out with me and Bonnie on Friday night? That would give us more time together."

More time together was what I was trying to avoid, so I made an excuse about a dinner date I just didn't want to break.

"Oh, yeah?" Corey's eyes lit up. I can't explain him, but Corey was happiest when he knew that his friends were sleeping around. And sleeping with your own husband or wife just didn't count. Sex had to be illicit, according to Corey, or you got no points for it.

"This guy you're having dinner with. Anyone I should know about?"

"I'll let you know on Saturday."

Saturday morning I got up at some ridiculous hour and got myself on that ridiculous Toonerville Trolley known as the Long Island Railroad. You've heard it all, I'm sure, about the wonderful trains in Japan, England, and Europe, and so how come we have such lousy trains in the U.S.? And if we can put a man on the moon, how come it takes close to three hours to go by train the one hundred miles from New York to Southampton? But that's what it does take, and by the time I got off that non-air-conditioned coach that bumped along the tracks at a speedy thirty miles an hour, I was wishing I had stayed in my air-conditioned apartment in New York.

Corey and Bonnie were waiting for me at the station. Corey was pushing sixty and trying to look like flaming youth in hip-hugging jeans, open shirt, silver chain around his neck, and gray hair that could have used a haircut about three weeks ago. That and a pointy gray beard gave him the appearance of a devil. Not a benevolent one, either.

Bonnie, who was pushing twenty-seven, wore the briefest shorts ever seen even in a beach community, a minuscule halter, and the highest-heeled mules ever made. Her pale blonde hair was frizzed into a halo around her head, but like Corey, she was no angel.

We got into the best rental car Avis could provide, and while Corey drove, Bonnie filled me in on the argument they had been having just before I arrived. It seems that Bonnie, who is bone-thin, model-thin, had decided to have an operation which would remove her two bottom ribs, one on each side of her rib cage.

Now, why did this blonde airhead want to go through all the pain and agony of such an operation? Haven't you heard? You look much thinner without those two bottom ribs which poke out your T-shirt and make your waistline look larger. Listening to Bonnie, the weekend loomed before me endlessly. Corey had told me how intelligent Bonnie was; she had gone to Bennington, briefly, of course, because she was too much for even that liberal school. But she wrote wonderful poetry, said Corey and was a great cook. "You should taste her oeufs à la neige." And she was built like a gazelle.

A cooking gazelle who wrote poetry—that's what I was condemned to for an entire weekend, and all because I was trying to distract myself from that married man, Andrew Lang. It seemed like too high a price to pay.

We arrived at the shabby cottage on Peconic Bay that Corey had rented for himself and his true love.

Bonnie indicated that she was not exactly happy with the Salvation Army castoffs with which the house was furnished, but she was sacrificing for Corey. Corey had told me one day over a five-martini lunch—he had consumed four of those martinis to my one—that he was having a hard time supporting Bonnie and her five-year-old daughter from an earlier liaison while at the same time sending money to Mrs. Eldon. I had never met Mrs. E., but I gather she was no longer a gazelle, being approximately the same age as Corey.

Bonnie took me to my room, this one done in Early Volunteers of America rejects, and I changed into white jeans—those blue jeans are just too much of a uniform for me—and a white shirt. The house did have one thing to recommend it: a screened porch with a great view of the bay and the sailboats skimming across the water. As long as you stayed outside the house, it was bearable. Corey and Bonnie were on the porch drinking vodka-and-tonics with their other guest, Mike Malloy, the Chicago TV writer.

To my surprise, he wasn't bad. He was around forty, actually well-dressed, a big change from most of Corey's friends who had never gotten over Woodstock. He was nice-looking and seemed amused by Bonnie, but hardly entranced.

He appeared to be a real friend to Corey, and it was the first time I had ever heard Corey in genuine conversation with another man, a conversation that did not revolve around drugs or who was going to bed with whom, and what they did once they got there.

"I guess you know Corey was a terrific writer some years back," Mike said to me after Corey had gone in to help his gazelle fix lunch.

"No, I didn't know." The only thing I knew about Corey was that he edited one of the pedestrian women's magazines that I wrote for.

"Sure, his stuff is in some of those short-story anthologies. You just have to go back a ways to find it, but he did some good stuff."

What happened, I wondered, between the good stuff and the junk that Corey was working on now? I liked Mike Malloy for being loyal to an old friend, and I liked him even more when, as we were eating tuna sandwiches on white bread with an exotic garnish of iceberg lettuce, he said that he'd take us all out to dinner that night.

Bonnie brightened at that—I guess she only liked making oeufs à la neige for Corey—but she said that instead of dinner, why didn't we go discoing instead?

"Sure," Mike said, "whatever you say."

That left the rest of the afternoon to get through. What do people do on a sunny day in Southampton? They go to the beach, right? Wrong. They go to Job's Lane, if they're visiting Bonnie, and go in and out of every shop on that boutique-lined street.

Corey bought and bought, but by the middle of the block it was clear he was running out of money.

"Mike and I are going to stop in here and have a drink," he said, when we had arrived in front of a pub called the Driver's Seat. "You two girls go ahead."

Bonnie made a little face. She was losing the chancellor of the exchequer, but then she seemed to think of something. Maybe she had a credit card or two in the tiny, fringed leather bag she wore over her shoulder.

88

"Okay," she said, "we'll see you in a little bit. Come on, Martine."

I went along with Bonnie and we ambled into a shop called the Voyager. Bonnie picked up an armload of bikini bathing suits and insisted I go into a dressing room with her. Once inside, I learned why she wanted me along. She pawed through the suits and handed me a tiny cream-and-maroon bikini.

"Here," she said, "this is the one I want. Put it under your jeans and shirt, Martine, and we'll sneak it out of here."

"What!"

"I'd do it myself, but I'm not wearing enough. It would show."

"Bonnie, you're crazy. If you want that suit, why don't you just buy it?"

"Because I don't have any money. Corey doesn't give me anything, Martine, and I need clothes."

Before bathing-suit weather came along I remembered that Corey had bought Bonnie three-hundred-dollar boots, two-hundred-fifty-dollar shoes from Jourdan's, and enough clothes to fill a closet.

"Oh sure," I said. "I'm walking back to the Driver's Seat, Bonnie. Are you coming?"

Bonnie laughed. Her scheme to get a new bathing suit without paying for it hadn't worked, but she wasn't mad. She took the suit to the cashier and paid for it with the credit card she had had with her all along.

"Have you tried it on?" the saleswoman asked. "Bathing suits aren't returnable."

Bonnie shrugged. "It's too hot to try things on. It'll be okay."

We walked back to the Driver's Seat, and once we

were seated in the open patio in the back drinking strawberry daiquiris she regaled Corey and Mike with what she called the "bikini heist."

"It would have been fun," she said, "only Martine wouldn't go along with it."

"Martine," Corey shook his head. "I guess every body has to have one square friend, and you're mine."

Big joke. Well, I wasn't about to give a lecture on Thou shalt not steal, not when I thought of Andy Lang. I concentrated on Mike Malloy. Here he was, available, interested, fairly amusing, and nice-looking. Why not him instead of Andy? It made much more sense.

We spent the rest of the afternoon drinking those strawberry daiquiris, and I didn't feel drunk, just slightly sick, as though I had been eating candy for too many hours.

I couldn't believe it when Corey downed his final daiquiri and said, "Cocktail time. Let's go back to the house."

"Cocktail time? But it's been cocktail time all afternoon."

"You can't call these things cocktails, Martine. We've been drinking the juice of a few berries. Let's go home for the real thing."

The real thing was vodka martinis, Andy's favorite drink. Remembering that, I joined cocktail time. The first one made me feel good, and the second one made Mike Malloy look good. I asked him to tell me what he did in TV. I remember nodding and listening, and I suppose I asked the appropriate questions at the appropriate times. I can't tell you what Mike answered because those martinis do nothing for my memory. At least nothing for my memory about the television in dustry, but I can recollect what happened between Mike and me.

Martini after martini disappeared, and Corey and Bonnie made some sounds about going out to dinner later.

"There's this place that has wonderful lobsters," Corey was saying. "Bonnie and me are going to take a nap, and when we get up we'll go for lobsters. That okay with everybody?"

"Fine," Mike said.

"You two be able to amuse yourselves?" Corey asked.

That Corey. He could make the simplest question hold at least three meanings.

"We'll be fine," Mike said.

Corey and Bonnie disappeared, and Mike and I sat on the porch looking out over Peconic Bay. The martinis were making me feel woozy, and the idea of a nap was appealing, I told Mike.

"Your room or mine?" he said.

"What?"

"I think your room is closer, but mine has a double bed."

Of course he was joking, but the martinis had left me without a flip reply, so I just said I would take a nap alone.

"Are you kidding?" He looked surprised. "Why would you want to do that?"

"Why do you want to sleep with me?"

"Because you're here, I'm here, and there's nothing better to do."

He wasn't kidding. "But we don't even know each other," I said.

That made him laugh. "You're something out of the Middle Ages. Look, I don't necessarily want to know you, except in a carnal sense, as they say in the good book. Besides, what has knowing each other got to do with going to bed?"

He was talking one language and I was talking another. He reminded me of Dee Dee. I stood up.

"If you ever come to the city, Mike, I have a girl-friend you might like to meet. See you later." And I left the porch and headed for the stairs.

"Jesus," Mike said.

I threw myself down on the bed—how nice that I had gotten the bed with the clean sheets—and fell into a heavy sleep for about two hours. When I came downstairs Corey and Bonnie were already sitting on the porch.

"Where's Mike?" Corey asked.

"I don't know. I guess in his room."

"No he's not. The door to his room is open, and he isn't there."

"I don't know. I went upstairs for a nap about two hours ago and I left him down here."

"You left him down here? Martine," Corey said, "you're hopeless."

Well, that's how the world goes. Twenty-five years ago if a woman jumped in and out of bed people would shake their heads and cluck their tongues and look disapproving. Now, if a woman doesn't jump in and out of bed people shake their heads and cluck their tongues and look disapproving.

"It's all for you, Corey. I don't want to do anything that would leave you without a single square friend to your name."

Corey laughed, and there was more talk about going out for dinner, trying the place with the wonderful lobsters, and wondering when Mike would get back. An hour went by, and it seemed clear that Mike probably wasn't coming back—at least not in time for dinner.

Corey drove us to the wonderful place for lobsters, and it was one of the most disgusting places I had ever seen. The restaurant was located on Shinnecock Bay. That part was nice. As for the rest of it, they didn't take reservations, which meant waiting at the bar for a table, and on a Saturday night the wait was at least three martinis long. We were finally seated at a wooden table at which the waitress took only a tentative swipe with a gray cloth. There were still bits of lobster shell imbedded in the wood grain when she had finished.

We ordered the wonderful lobster, which tasted like steamer clams. The cooks evidently used the same pot of boiling water for everything they prepared. If the lobster tasted of clams, the corn on the cob tasted of lobster and the salad tasted of iceberg lettuce, which it was.

None of us finished our lobsters, and Corey did say something about taking the leftover lobster home for a lobster salad for lunch tomorrow, but Bonnie vetoed that.

"What a disgusting idea."

After dinner Corey suggested that we visit a few bars and one or two discos to look for Mike.

"You two go ahead," I said, "I've had a long day. You know what it's like traveling for three hours first thing in the morning on the Long Island Railroad."

"Well," Corey said, "if you're really tired. What do you say, Bonnie? I'm a little tired myself."

Bonnie looked at him with alarm. "But it's Saturday. And it's only eleven o'clock."

Corey rallied. "Right! Too early to go home. But we'll take you home first, Martine, and then we'll go on from there."

"I could call a cab," I said.

"Don't be silly," said Mr. Gallantry. He wouldn't let me take a cab, but he would let me take care of the dinner check. It was all because the place didn't take credit cards, and Mike was supposed to take us out to dinner, and I had messed that up, and besides, I didn't mind, did I?

I never minded taking Corey and his lady friends out for dinner. In New York it was lunch, and it was the little kickback that all his writers gave Corey for their regular monthly assignments. It was a small price, smaller than an agent's fee, and far cheaper than some of the demands made by other editors. I would still like to sell the oil painting of Venice foisted on me by one editor who fancied himself an artist; compared to that, what was an occasional dinner or a monthly lunch?

Corey and Bonnie drove me back to the house, and I sat on the porch for a while trying to see something interesting in the black water and the star-filled black sky. I went upstairs after a bit and never did hear Corey and Bonnie and Mike come in.

I started looking at the railroad timetable on Sunday morning before I went downstairs for breakfast. What was the earliest train I could take, I wondered, without insulting Corey?

When I walked into the kitchen, Corey was sitting at the table looking as though he didn't care about trains or timetables or anything else.

"What a night," he said. "We found Mike at one disco and then we went on to another. And another. Or was it two others? I lost track."

I looked around the kitchen and wondered if there was a coffee pot, or coffee to put into it. The martinis I had had the night before made me yearn for orange juice.

"Is Bonnie up?" I asked Corey.

"Bonnie won't be up for hours."

"Let's you and me go into town for coffee. What do you say, Corey?"

"I'll go with you anywhere, Martine, especially for coffee. But you have to drive."

The two of us drove into the village and stopped at a coffee shop at the corner of Job's Lane called Act IV, a cute place decorated with theatrical posters and featuring ice cream sundaes named after old Broadway musicals. I winced when I saw that the Porgy and Bess sundae was chocolate ice cream with hot fudge sauce, but other than that the place was okay.

It took two cups of black coffee for Corey to be able to open his eyes, and a third cup for him to start lecturing me on the way I was wasting my life. It was a waste, according to Corey, because I never went to bed with anybody. I thought of Peregrine and Andy, but I didn't have to make Corey my confidant. Besides, I could stand his disapproval a lot easier than his leering enjoyment of the truth.

"Mike is a nice guy," he said. "You missed a good bet with Mike. I've seen him. He's really hung."

I always knew what Corey was trying to do when he spoke to me that way. He hoped to see me wince or whimper or look shocked. I never did any of those

95

things. I did what I always did when Corey tried his shock tactics. I looked interested.

"Really? Tell me about it, Corey."

He laughed, paid for the coffee, and said, "Let's go back to the house."

Corey, the little devil, had a surprise waiting for me at the house. He hadn't told me about it over coffee because he hoped that if he couldn't shock me one way, he could shock me another. Mike was supposed to have that effect on me. Mike and the tall blonde woman who came down the stairs with him after Corey and I had been sitting on the porch for an hour or so.

"Good morning," Mike said. "Martine, you haven't met—" he turned to the tall blonde, "—what *is* your name, honey?"

She laughed. "God, you're a bad man. It's Patricia Simmons."

"Everybody meet Patricia."

"We met last night," Corey said. He turned to me. "But you haven't met Patricia. They met last night while doing the hustle. Or was it the boogie?"

I waved, "Hi, Patricia."

She put her arm on Mike's before she spoke, "And what's your name, dear?"

"Jane Austen."

Mike laughed and Corey shook his head.

"Jane, you should have been with us. We had the best time. First we went to L'Oursin, and then we went to Les Mouches, and finally we ended up at the St. James Hotel."

"No, finally we ended up here," Mike said. "In my bed built for two." He disengaged his arm from Patricia's. "And where are you staying, Pat honey? Would you like me to run you home?"

"I'd like some coffee first," Patricia said. "I'm grouping with some people in Hampton Bays, and no one ever makes coffee."

"No one makes it here, either," Corey said. "We just came back from having coffee in town."

"Why don't we stop for coffee on the way home?" Mike asked.

"Sure," she shrugged. Clearly she knew you couldn't win them all. "Goodbye, Corey. Nice meeting you, Jane."

"So long, Pat."

Corey waited until Mike and Patricia had driven off. "Jane Austen. You're a terrible snob, Martine."

"It comes with the territory, Corey."

I called my mother when I got home from Southampton.

"Did you have a nice time?" she asked.

"Sure. It was okay."

"Just okay?"

"Well, Corey is crazy, his girlfriend is crazy, and the man they introduced me to wanted me to go to bed with him because he said there was nothing better to do."

"What a romantic approach," my mother said, "I hope you pushed him right into Peconic Bay."

"Nope. I just told him that if he didn't watch out, my mother would be waiting for him back in New York with a shotgun."

My mother laughed. "I'm glad you have a sense of humor about it."

"That's life in the big city, Mom. You get used to it."

"It wasn't always that way," my mother said.

"I know. You used to dance with Scott and Zelda in the Plaza fountain, and then you'd have pancakes at Child's after a wild night in a speakeasy."

"That was before my time," my mother said. "You read too many books, Martine, and you romanticize things."

"I romanticize things? Then why did you just say that things weren't the way they are now?"

"I meant that people were different, Marty. I knew people who slept around, too, but it was different—I don't know, more romantic, somehow."

I thought about my father who had pursued my mother across three continents, until they married, finally, in New York City.

"Mom, you know how Daddy followed you from Europe to the United States via South America? Well, today a man won't take a girl out if she lives in the Bronx. And just forget it if she lives in Brooklyn."

"Well, at least you live in Manhattan."

"That's not what I mean."

"I know what you mean. You think I don't know what you mean? Anyway, I'm glad you went to Southampton. You never know—"

"—if you don't go," I finished up for her.

My mother was silent, and then, "I just want you to be happy, Marty. You're so alone. I don't want you to be so alone."

"I'm not alone," I said. "I've got you. I've got my work. I've got my friends."

"That's not what I'm talking about," my mother

said. "It's nice, but it's not enough. Your mother and your friends, work—nice, but not for a whole life."

"You're afraid I'm going to be an old maid? Don't worry, I've been married once. I'm not a complete failure."

"You're not a failure at all." My mother's voice was sharp. "You're my beautiful, successful child. I just want you to be with someone, Marty, to have someone. Your father and I loved Davy, too. I want to know that you have someone now. That's all I care about."

"A girl's best friend is her mother," I said, trying to lighten the sky.

"Oh, Marty," my mother said, "why can't you be like other American children? Why can't you learn to hate your mother?"

That made me laugh, and all the time my mother kept saying, "I don't see what's so funny, I really don't."

When I finally stopped laughing, my mother asked, shyly, "Are we going to have dinner together this week?"

Until this summer's romance, my mother and I always had dinner once or twice a week. My mother would come directly over from the department store where she worked, I would cook dinner, and she would spend the night. It was easier for her to go to work from my apartment than to go home late at night to Riverdale and then to have to leave early the following morning to get to her job. But with Andy in my life, my schedule had changed. I had never been so involved with anyone before, and I had never permitted anyone to stay in my apartment overnight. It changed the logistics, if not the relationship, between me and my mother.

"Of course we'll have dinner," I said.

"Shall I come over?" she asked. "When do you want me?"

Andy would return from Fire Island that night. Why should I keep my evening open for that very-married man? Because I wanted to, that's why.

"We'll talk tomorrow, Mom, okay?"

"Of course. Remember, Marty, I just want to see you happy, not alone. Just remember that."

She knew. My mother knew. But she never pried, for the simple reason that she meant it when she said she just wanted to see me happy. Other people might say those words, but my mother lived them.

CHAPTER XII

Andy

After that evening in Chinatown, I stopped fighting my feeling for Martine. I saw her almost every evening and spent most nights until early morning in her apartment.

There were some evenings when I had to go to a business dinner or visit some friends of mine and Janet's, but I would break away as soon as I could and go to Martine's.

One night I couldn't get out of a dinner invitation at the Saylors'. Judy Saylor was a good friend of Janet's, and she made a good home-cooked meal. Judy and her husband, Stan, were spending their summer in New York, and this was their fifth invitation to dinner. I had finally run out of excuses.

My evening with the Saylors was a disaster. Not that the food wasn't good. Our circle of friends took cooking very seriously. It was part of the upwardly mobile culture. Our heroes were Julia Child, Craig Claiborne, and the *Larousse Gastronomique*. It was all very fashionable. And if nothing else, Judy Saylor, a nice girl from the Bronx, was going to be fashionable. The Saylors lived in a fashionable duplex off Madison Avenue, on the fashionable East Side. The apartment was very expensively decorated, not by any ordinary department store, but by a professional, highly acclaimed designer. Judy's clothes were always the latest, and as rapidly as the media dictated change, she changed her wardrobe. She also had kids who could have made the best-dressed list.

All Judy and Stan did throughout the entire evening was argue about money, each trying to enlist my sympathies. I had wondered why the Saylors hadn't taken a house on Fire Island this summer, and now I knew. Stan's business was doing badly and showing no signs of improvement. I found out that evening that the Saylors were living off their savings and borrowing money besides.

Stan was right to be worried, but Judy ignored his financial complaints and kept pressing him.

"We need new drapes," she said, while I pretended great interest in the broiled chicken, "ours are almost two years old. And we need a bigger fridge. We do a lot of entertaining. And we really should have taken a house on Fire Island, even if only for one month. When Andy was out of a job a couple of years ago he and Janet rented a house on Fire Island for a month. Didn't you, Andy?"

"God, Judy, I don't remember. Maybe. Yeah. I guess so."

"Janet's terrific," Judy went on. "She knows how to get what she wants. I wish I were more like her."

"Shut up," Stan said. "Can't you understand that we just don't have the money?"

"Guys," I said, and my fork rattled against the plate, "I'm working on a new presentation and I brought a lot of work home. I've really got to be going."

The Saylors looked embarrassed, and Stan said, "Hey, Andy, I'm sorry. But you know what it's like when the money isn't coming in."

"Sure do," I said, remembering Janet's anger when I lost my job. Judy was a lot like her. "Things will turn around, Stan. They always do."

"They had better," Judy said, and then she and Stan walked me to the door, asking me to please come soon again.

"Sure," I said, "absolutely. I'll call you."

Once on the street I walked a block until I found a pay phone and called Martine.

"I know it's late," I said, "but could you spare a drink for a man who's just managed an escape act from a chamber of horrors?"

"If you get rid of the chains and the spider webs," Martine said, "you're welcome."

I grabbed a cab and was at her door in five minutes.

Martine greeted me at the door wearing a shimmering gold caftan, and her face glowed, showing she was happy to see me. Seeing her made me feel better and I embraced and kissed her with extra ardor and hunger. She responded happily and in kind, but she sensed that there was more in the kiss than sexual hunger.

"What's the matter?"

103

"I had to see you. I'll tell you all about it, but I need a drink first."

I was remembering back two years ago when I had lost my job. I had come home and told Janet, and she had lashed out with, "Why can't you keep a job?"

And Janet was Judy's role model. Some model.

I finished my drink and Martine insisted on making me another. She did, but with considerably less vodka. I was calming down. Being with Martine, her sympathy and loveliness and the cocoon that was her apartment, achieved the effect I wanted. When Martine saw that I was less occupied with the bitterness of the evening she disappeared only to reappear a moment later with a large box from Bergdorf Goodman tied with a white ribbon.

"I have a present for you," she said.

"A present for me? At eleven-thirty at night? What's the occasion? What's in it?" I was so surprised I didn't even reach for it.

"Take it and find out. The occasion is because you're here. And what's wrong with eleven-thirty at night for giving presents?"

I wanted to grab the box and tear it open but I restrained myself like a well-behaved, grownup person and reached out for it and placed the box in my lap. I coolly untied the ribbon, took off the top, pushed the tissue paper aside and took out a garment and held it in front of me. It was a man's robe but it was more than a robe. It was a gaily colored, striped silk caftan.

"I know how uncomfortable you are in clothes," she said. "So when you come here in the evenings or to spend the night, you can be comfortable. Why don't you try it on?"

I did. It felt so good. The silk against my body was very nice. My robes were always terrycloth because they were floppy, useful, and comfortable. But this was luxurious. I preened like a peacock and beamed.

"Why don't you put your hands in the pockets?"

I did and found a small envelope. It had my name on it.

"More?"

"Open it and see."

Inside the envelope was a silver Tiffany key ring with a key, plus a card which read *Mi casa es su casa*.

It wasn't my birthday, Christmas, Valentine's Day. It wasn't even Martin Van Buren Day. It was Tuesday, eleven-thirty, mid-July, that's all. And it was a good reason for Martine to give me a gift.

Lovemaking was especially sweet that night, and the bad taste of the evening was gone.

I spent every moment I could with Martine. Not only evenings, but we'd manage to meet for lunch when we could. We talked on the phone several times a day, sometimes for just a minute. It was brief, but it was like touching hands. I had my work which kept me away from her, and the weekends, which were becoming onerous to me. I really wanted to be with Martine but I also wanted to see my kids. I didn't want to see Janet, but I was afraid she might be hearing things about my activities in the city.

When I got off the ferry at Fire Island on Friday evening I would look into Janet's face, trying to determine the mood she was in. If she looked grim it could be because she was suspicious or it could be because of the kids. I always reassured myself that she couldn't know about Martine because Janet was on Fire Island

and I was in New York. Yet one Friday evening after the girls were put to bed she asked, "Where were you last night?"

"Last night? Why?"

"I called you last night until midnight and you weren't home. The answering machine wasn't on, either."

By the time she answered my "why" I had rallied and prepared my answer. I told her about the new business pitch we were making and my important role in it. I told her how much work was involved. I even embellished the explanation with gossip about Bart Mitchell, my boss with whom I was spending a lot of time.

I hoped all this personal detail would make my story plausible and satisfy Janet. I silently cursed myself for forgetting to turn on the answering machine. I had to be more careful.

CHAPTER XIII

Martine

I think of myself as a fairly sane and sensible person. Practical in large matters, though not necessarily in small ones. Why, then, did I agree to the idea that Andy move in with me for the summer? We discussed it so sanely and sensibly, too. It was only going to be for the summer. When his wife and children returned from Fire Island, he would return to their apartment. But meanwhile, what was the sense in going home late at night? Why leave my warm bed to return to his empty one? Why not just bring a few things over to my apartment and stay there overnight. It was the practical thing to do. That's what we told ourselves.

It was also wonderful. My mother tells me that I wasn't really a child when I was a child. I was too serious. I'd had a happy time with Davy, but that was just a little bit of happiness many years before. With Andy I was a child again. We were two happy children playing hooky and we knew it couldn't last, but we would enjoy our fun for the rest of the summer and then become responsible adults in September.

It all started when I gave him a robe and a key to the apartment. And then he said that he might as well bring over a shirt and another tie. And what about another suit? And how about his shaving stuff? And how could he stay even one night without a comb? And then when all that was in my apartment, why bother going home to his?

Summer is the only possible time for acting out this kind of fantasy, because it's the time when so many people are out of town. His friends, my friends, his family. Besides, in this year of our Lord who cares about who's sleeping with whom? You'd be surprised. A lot of people care, people you hardly notice. Let's start with:

The doormen and the superintendent.

"Your friend is upstairs," Bill the doorman would tell me, quite unasked.

"The management likes to know who has keys to the apartments," Mr. Hunt, the superintendent said.

Then there are the neighbors.

"Is that nice-looking gentleman your fiance?" Mrs. Crow, my next-door neighbor, asked me one night at the incinerator.

And then, one afternoon Andy had an envelope of papers delivered by messenger from one of his clients, and the messenger went to the wrong apartment.

"I think that people have no right to have things delivered here if they don't live here," the harpy who had received the envelope by mistake screamed at me. "I think they should take out a post office box and not

108

bother decent people who have to be constantly open-ing the door to messengers who could rape a person!''

There were very few friends of mine who knew about Andy at that time. But those few made their own comments.

Dee Dee: "It will never work. He'll leave and make you miserable, and you'll be sorry you ever got involved with him."

Alicia: (practically salivating after she and her husband met Andy for the first time) "Is he married? I bet he's married. I told Larry that I bet he's married."

Corey: (after he saw us at a restaurant) "He looks like he could be a real bad boy, Martine. Is he? How about the four of us—me and Bonnie, you and your old man—getting together one night? Wouldn't that be fun?"

"No."

"No?"

"No."

"Oh. Okay, then, how about having lunch with me and Harriet tomorrow at La Veranda."

"Harriet? Who's Harriet? Where's Bonnie?"

"You'll love Harriet, she's Greek. I call her my Peloponnesian Poppy. Bonnie is in Massachusetts visiting her mother. Want to bring your friend to lunch?"

"No thanks."

"But you'll be there?"

It was time to pick up a lunch check. "I'll be there."

If there was anything Andy and I didn't want during those first few weeks it was to be with other people. He would come home after work—to my home, our home—and I'd run to greet him at the door. Working at home gave me the time during the day to do the marketing and to cook little goodies for Andy. I spoiled him because I loved him and I enjoyed doing for him.

He called me his geisha, and I liked that, too. Independent me, hardworking me, self-sufficient me. I liked being Andy's geisha. Had I been Davy's geisha? It worried me that I couldn't remember. It worried me that I was doing more, giving more to Andy, than I had given to Davy. At least that's the way I remembered it. When I was married to Davy, he had done for me, taken care of me. How had the tables turned so? I should have done more for Davy, I should be doing less for Andy. Andy didn't deserve all I was doing, while Davy had deserved everything.

The thoughts kept nagging at me, but I kept telling myself it was only for the summer, and meanwhile I liked doing things for Andy. The simplest things thrilled him: he went crazy over a hot fudge ice cream sundae, and he nibbled on my fingers after I had rubbed the crust of rye bread slices with garlic.

We had most of our dinners in bed. We would eat, watch television, sip wine, and make love. The lovemaking that was so wonderful at the beginning got better as it went along. We only disagreed over Andy's penchant for being an early bird. He thought that six A.M. was the middle of the day. I would feel him caressing me at five A.M. and I thought the man was mad. One morning over coffee, I suggested that he come home for lunch.

"Around one o'clock would be best," I told him.

"One o'clock? Why?"

"Because in the words of the song: 'That's my time of day, and you're the only one I want to share it with.' "

110

He grinned but he came, and after that it was often one P.M. as well as five A.M., and that was all right with me.

Sometimes Andy would call me from his office and we would meet at a restaurant, a bar, or our first meeting place, the Central Park Zoo. We were walking through there one soft and early summer evening when we came upon the bear cage. The bears were cuddling and touching and about to make love.

"Let's not watch them," Andy said. "Let's give them their privacy."

We turned away and walked to the seal pond where Andy gave some remarkable barks that sent the seals swimming to our side of the pool. *Davy*, I thought, *oh Davy*.

"That's wonderful," I said, "I love that."

"That's nothing," he said. "I can also coo like a dove."

"No!"

"And you should hear me as a frog."

"Not that, too!"

"Absolutely. My kids love it when I make animal sounds. One summer in Fire Island they had a pack of their friends over, and I made each kid pretend to be a musical instrument, and then I imitated those instruments for them. They went crazy."

"I bet."

We walked out of Central Park and I was thinking that it was all pretend, everything about us, and the sooner the summer was over the better it would be. This wasn't just a married man. This was a married man with kids, kids whom he adored. Kids he cooed to, kids for whom he played Tubby the Tuba. We were

111

acting like children, but we certainly weren't children. Andy had children. Could a child have a child? And once you have a child, you have to put childish things away from you. I finally understood the meaning of that sentence from the Bible.

There was a time for all things, and there was no time for me and Andy. If we had met years before, things would have been different. But now it was entirely too late. Too bad, but that's how it was.

"I'd like to buy you a really elegant dinner," Andy said, and I knew he was thinking what I had been thinking. "Where would you like to go? Some place quiet and expensive, or some place splashy and expensive?"

"Splashy and expensive," I said immediately.

Quiet and expensive sounded too much like something out of *Back Street*, and that was not the way I wanted to see myself. When things ended between us, I wanted it to be with a bang, not a whimper.

CHAPTER XIV

Andy

Boy, was I careful. I made certain I left Martine's key in the office. I never carried it around for fear I would accidentally bring it to Fire Island. Each morning I would check my clothes to make certain there were no stray hairs of Martine's on me. When Martine and I were out together, I tried to find places my crowd didn't go. I was glad I didn't have a doorman to see me arrive each morning at dawn and politely inquire how Mrs. Lang and the little girls were. The doormen at Martine's house had begun to recognize me as a regular visitor and they would let me pass without announcing me through the building intercom. But they were discreet. They never seemed to smirk. When I entered the building they always greeted me with "Good evening, sir," and let me pass. In a building with hundreds of apartments I supposed there were many episodes like mine going on.

One evening after work I met Martine at the Carlyle for drinks. It was a comfortable bar with a piano player who liked Gershwin as much as I did. I also felt we wouldn't be likely to run into anybody I knew there because it wasn't an in-place. It was never crowded. So far I had not run into anybody I knew at the public places where we had gone. So I kept pressing my luck.

It didn't work this time. It's absolutely amazing to me that in a city the size of New York with all its millions of people I could run into somebody I knew, but it could have been worse. The man waving from a nearby table was Jim O'Donnell with a friend he introduced as Ilona. While Jim was a good friend of mine and we had met Martine at the same time, I was not too happy to see him. I never told him I was seeing Martine. Actually, I never discussed Martine with anyone.

At first I was startled to be discovered by someone I knew, but I quickly relaxed because it was only Jim and Ilona, not Jim's wife. She wasn't even the boss's secretary, whom I knew he had been seeing.

I asked Jim and Ilona to join us for a drink. Jim beamed. He recognized Martine. He looked at both of us and said, "So, you've been seeing each other behind my back, have you?"

"No," I said laughing nervously. "We've just met for drinks. You know I've been working like hell on that coffee account. Who's got time?"

Jim laughed and actually winked at me. He introduced Ilona and added, "Martine, you and Ilona should get to know each other. You're a writer and Ilona's an editor."

"Oh, books or magazines?"

"Magazines. *Fashion Interiors*."

"No wonder we haven't run into each other. I've never written for them. It's not a field I've ever gotten involved with."

"Well, if you're ever interested in writing for us, call me and maybe we can arrange for an assignment."

Ilona was a large shapely girl, fleshy, with a very prominent bosom and short, cropped red hair. Ilona's big breasts would be Jim's delight. He prided himself on being a tit man. All the girls he was attracted to had big bosoms. Ilona was also sweet and pleasant and was apparently quite taken with Jim. Given their familiarity with each other and references to other times and places, it was clear they had obviously been seeing each other for some time.

Martine and I deliberately kept the conversation mostly on Jim and Ilona, movies, office stories, even the latest event reported in the *Times*, but away from us.

Finally Jim said, "How about the four of us having dinner together? I know a great new Thai restaurant that just opened on Eighth Avenue."

Naturally he was experienced enough to pick an obscure, out-of-the-way place.

"They're so new," he added, "they haven't even got a liquor license, so we'll have to bring our own wine."

Martine didn't seem too enthusiastic about the idea. She said something about Thai food being too hot. I thought it was a good idea and with enough pleading and cajoling from the three of us, Martine was persuaded to go along.

At the restaurant Martine seemed withdrawn, but I

115

ignored her. Jim was very expansive and insisted on ordering for all of us. He had picked up some cheap Spanish wine along the way. It turned out to be sour. He tried to start friendly conversations with the waiters who smiled and nodded politely, but it was clear they could barely understand English. Jim kept repeating what luck that we had run into each other, and since we were all having such a good time the four of us should arrange to meet more often. He even recommended a specific date for our next get-together. I could see Martine began to squirm and start lame excuses. So I said we'd check our calendars, that I would get back to him the next day, and that settled him for a while.

As expansive as Jim was as a host, he let me pick up the check. As we were leaving he made one last bid for a date to meet again, and even suggested next Wednesday. I said I would let him know, and we parted.

Martine was unusually silent in the cab going back to her apartment. When we got inside the apartment I reached to take her in my arms because we were finally alone. I was feeling pretty good. Jim had been in good form, Ilona had been pleasant, and I was pleased to have spent the evening with them and Martine.

But Martine walked away from my outstretched arms, lit a cigarette, and sat in a chair at the opposite side of the room. I could see she was angry with me and had been so since we left the restaurant. Martine was always affectionate and tactile. Whenever we were in a cab she would nestle close to me. In the cab ride home she sat at the other end of the seat looking out the window. Now she was puffing rapidly on a cigarette like a campy Bette Davis. Martine didn't smoke.

"What's wrong?" I asked.

"You don't know?"

"No, I don't. But if it's something I've done, you'd better let me know."

"Better? All right, you asked for it. We were going to spend the evening together, just the two of us. Then along comes your good friend, Don Juan with his little bimbo, and we end up spending the evening with them listening to his jokes, drinking his sour wine. Then he suggests we're all a jolly foursome, with me being your little piece. Well, let me tell you. I'm not Ilona and I'm not your little piece just out for a good time with a married man."

"But you seemed to enjoy yourself," I protested. "You laughed a lot during the evening."

"What would you have me do, walk out in the middle of dinner? I tried to tell you at the Carlyle I didn't want to go, but you didn't get the message. Don't you see, Andy? I just wanted to be with you."

I stood there shifting from foot to foot feeling foolish and stupid. I didn't agree with her about Jim. But I didn't want her to be angry with me. I walked over to her and put my hands on her shoulders hoping I could ease her anger, but she shrugged them off. Then I became angry. She was unreasonable.

"Look. Jim is a good friend of mine. The fact that he plays around a lot is his business, not yours or mine. And one reason I like him is he doesn't judge. And don't you judge. He enjoyed being with us and I enjoyed being with him. I thought you did too. If you didn't you should have said so."

117

I felt I was being attacked unfairly for being friendly with Jim as well as for reasons Martine wasn't revealing. I tried to placate her. I knelt by the side of the chair and took her hand.

"If you're upset we weren't alone I can understand that, and I'm truly sorry. I know it's difficult for us. And the fact that we ran into somebody, well, it was inevitable. But wasn't it lucky it was Jim?"

She tugged her hand away from mine. "Don't you understand what happened tonight? Don't you understand what he thinks of me—and Ilona too, for that matter? And you went along with him. Is that what I am to you?"

I stood up not knowing what to say. I didn't understand what she was talking about. She watched me for a while, then got up from her chair, put out the cigarette, and said, "Look, Andy, I'm not feeling well. I've got an early morning meeting with an editor to go over a new assignment. I'm going to take a sleeping pill and go to bed."

She gently but firmly led me to the door, gave me a perfunctory kiss, said "Call me tomorrow" and shut the door behind me.

She was so angry she sent me home. This would be the first evening in weeks I didn't spend with her, the first night we wouldn't make love. I got home and seethed. There's nothing like being attacked unfairly to give one a sense of righteous indignation, and I felt righteous and indignant. I turned on the television set in the empty apartment and started watching the late show, but all I saw was a replay of the evening. I tried to pick out the scene that triggered Martine's anger but I couldn't. As I re-created the evening, all I could

118

determine was that we had had a good time, even thought the wine was sour and the food too spicy. Now my anger began to build because Martine was wrong. She was temperamental and unpredictable and she didn't like my friends. Maybe it was better to find all that out now. God knows what else she's like. Maybe I was lucky to know all this before I got in any deeper.

With these new discoveries I began to feel a sense of relief and I went to bed. I didn't sleep. Instead I twisted and turned, continuing to go over in my head what Martine said I had done. There had to be something, but it kept eluding me. I finally poured a very large whiskey and was able to sleep after I drank it.

In the morning I knew my righteous resolutions of the night before just wouldn't do. Right or wrong I wanted to continue seeing Martine. I called her from the office because I wanted to be sure I didn't wake her. She seemed glad to hear from me, and that pleased me. This had been our first fight and it had made me miserable and unhappy. And we hadn't had the opportunity to kiss and make up.

"Martine, I'm sorry about last night," I blurted out. I still wasn't sure what I had done, but if she was so hurt maybe I had been wrong.

"I am too, Andy."

Just hearing her say that made me feel happy and relieved. I was sure we would kiss and make up that night.

CHAPTER XV

Martine

Life can be beautiful, or so it seemed when Andy and I were together, just the two of us. It was the appearance of other people that caused the trouble. Like Andy's fathead friend Jim O'Donnell. Andy and I met at the Carlyle for drinks one night, and who should we run into but Jim and his more-or-less-permanent on-the-sly girlfriend Ilona Smith.

Of course, Jim insisted that we all sit together for a drink, and of course, my Andy had to agree. Do I hear someone out there asking what's wrong with that?

I'll tell you. First, Jim was getting a big charge out of catching Andy in the act. We could have been as innocent as Mary's little lamb, but we weren't, so we both acted guilty and sly, and I almost killed Andy when he felt he had to make a dozen dumb explanations as to why we were having a drink together.

That made the guilt and everything we were about

even more crystal-clear to Jim. He was off with his not-so-clever double entendres and his macho act of what big men he and Andy were, having two such pretty bimbos on the side.

Poor Ilona—that's how I always thought of her after that—didn't seem to mind. It was obvious that she was gone and gaga on Jim, and anything he did and said was all right with her. I could see the way she looked at him that she thought there was some kind of future there, some idea in the back of her dyed red head that one day Jim would leave his Irish Catholic wife and his four Irish Catholic children and explain to his Irish Catholic mother and father that he was getting a divorce to marry that other woman.

That was Poor Ilona's problem, true. But the more time we spent together, it became clear that Jim was also sure that it was Poor Martine's problem as well, and he just about strutted and crowed, and said in everything but words, "We're quite the boys, aren't we?"

If the meeting with Jim and Poor Ilona could have ended there I suppose I would have calmed down in time, but then Jim suggested that we all have dinner together at some little Thai restaurant on Eighth Avenue, and Andy agreed.

I tried to make the best of it, honest injun, I did. But the moment I saw that restaurant I felt as though I was hurting all over. I wanted to go home and pull the covers over my head. Talk about back street—you can't get much further back than Eighth Avenue!

Jim continued his smirky, leering looks and his clever remarks throughout the evening. At least he thought they were clever. Jim, the Noel Coward of the suburbs.

Somewhere between the minced fish balls and the spicy cabbage bits Jim came out with his suggestion of the evening.

"Andy," he said, "we've got to do this again. But next time, let's make it the six of us."

"Six?" Andy asked. And I was wondering if Jim was planning to include their wives. But Jim had a better idea than that.

"Sure. We'll get Bill Mitchell to come along. You know. And we'll tell him to bring his friend."

For *friend* read mistress, girl, other woman. I could see the evening that Jim had planned. Three men—three married men—parading their mistresses for each other's approval.

This is the girl I sleep with when the wife's away. What do you think of her? A pretty nice piece, right? And wait till I tell you what she does for me in bed. Things my wife would never do.

Very Victorian or Edwardian or something out of Schnitzler's turn-of-the-century Vienna. Except that this was New York, late twentieth century, and you'd think women had progressed beyond that kind of treatment. And maybe if we haven't, it's our own fault. Because let me tell you Poor Ilona's dumb reaction.

"That's a wonderful idea," she fluttered at Jim. "I'd love to meet more of your friends."

She and I should have stood together and dumped that Thai food over Jim's head before marching out of that restaurant. But Poor Ilona thought it was wonderful, and I said nothing.

And Andy? He just shrugged and said, "Sure, we'll do that sometime."

Over my dead body.

123

And the worst of it was that Andy didn't understand why I was upset. We parted from Jim and Poor Ilona and went back to my apartment. Andy had moved some of his clothes to my place—why not? I had given him a key, but he didn't stay over every night. Andy returned to his own apartment to check the mail, rumple the bed convincingly for the maid, and change his clothes.

Andy was also a slave to his answering machine. Janet and the kids were never out of his mind. During the evening he used his beeper to check messages on his machine almost every hour on the hour. Well, guilt feelings are guilt feelings—you don't need to study Siggy Freud to know that.

The night we had dinner with friend Jim was one of the nights we were planning to spend together—completely together—until it was time for Andy to leave for work. But once we got back to my place I knew I didn't want him there. That evening had left me with a terrible feeling. Jim thought Poor Ilona was cheap. Was I sure that Andy didn't feel the same way about me? I wasn't sure at all. Maybe Martine was on her way to becoming Poor Martine. The idea made me sick.

Sick and tired. Too tired to embark on a scene with Andy. And what would be the point of it? I was becoming more aware that ours was the traditional summer romance, and summer was fast coming to an end.

"I think you better go home tonight, Andy," I said.

"What? Why?"

I just couldn't bear to explain. If he didn't catch the nuances of the situation, he wasn't sensitive to my feelings. And if he wasn't sensitive, I didn't want him around. Not that night. Maybe never.

"Go home, Andy, I'm tired. It's been a long day."

He left, and I took a quick shower and went to bed. It was wonderful being in bed by myself. I could relax, stretch catty-corner across the double bed, and I could return to my own schedule of watching the Late Show, the Late-Late Show, and the Late-Late-Late Show. A free-lancer makes her own schedule, and I was tired of adjusting my life to Andy's. I would go back to sleeping late in the morning and working late into the night.

An advertising man! What did I want with an advertising man? Peregrine always made fun of them, and I was beginning to see that Peregrine was right. He was right about a lot of things. He was a free-lance writer and I was a free-lance writer, and we had a lot in common. Besides, Peregrine didn't have a wife and two adorable little girls, and if he had a friend like Jim O'Donnell he had the sense never to introduce me to him.

I was paying the price for my infidelity to Davy. Davy's kindnesses, his tenderness, his love, memories came flooding over me. Knowing how I loved French chocolates, Davy had had a special stamp made up: *Cartier the Bonbonnière*, it said. He had then gone to Cartier the jeweler, bought a pair of earrings, wrapped them in heavy brown paper, and stamped the paper with the crazy stamp. This strange package was delivered to me by messenger, and when I opened it I found jewels rather than chocolate truffles.

I was lucky finally to be able to see things so clearly. Lucky not to be more involved with Andy. Because when you're less involved it's easier to say goodbye.

I was even lucky with the television fare that night: *The Maltese Falcon* on the Late Show, followed by *Casablanca* on the Late-Late show. It was a Humphrey Bogart festival. Only I cried like crazy when Ingrid got on that plane, leaving Humphrey forever, and at four A.M. I finally took a sleeping pill.

CHAPTER XVI

Martine

"Martine, hi, hope I didn't wake you?"

It was almost noon, and it was my friend Alicia O'Malley on the phone. Alicia is one of those people whom Dee Dee once described as "an old friend who we should maybe stop seeing, because just being an old friend is not enough of an excuse for being a bore."

For the most part I agreed with Dee Dee, and a lot of old friends were gone from my life. But Alicia was truly an old friend. Emphasis on the friend. She would die for me, if need be, or at least come to my rescue. I could call her at four A.M. if I had a problem, and I knew she'd be at my doorstep in fifteen minutes. The truth was that I had never called Alicia at four A.M. I just knew that I could.

Alicia was loving and irritating. We had known each other in college, and married within a few months of each other. After Davy died, Alicia was one of the few friends who had stayed lovingly close. A widow of twenty-three is an embarrassing bore to couples with children, but Alicia insisted that we could be friends forever, and if I didn't call her she made sure to keep in touch with me.

That was all very nice, but even though we loved each other our lives had taken very different paths. I was a widow living in Manhattan, and working. To Alicia, I was the most glamorous person she knew. She never said but implied that I was leading a wild and wonderful life. Alicia and Larry, meanwhile, had had two children, bought a comfortable house in the suburbs, and I suppose that my picture of Alicia's life was no more realistic than Alicia's picture of mine.

Alicia knew I always ate in the best restaurants, courtesy of divine escorts, had countless affairs, courtesy of divine men, and slept till at least three every day. On the whole, I preferred her version of "Martine, This is Your Life" to the version entertained by various cousins who lived smugly in New Jersey.

While Alicia often envied me—her life was comfortable, she admitted, but hardly exciting—my cousins pitied me. I was the only female member of our family who actually had to work for a living. True, one cousins did volunteer work for as much as six hours each day, and another did part-time work in a hospital when her life at home became too boring, a third started a little artsy-craftsy boutique, and a fourth got a part-time job as a receptionist for a dentist. But all were aware that they didn't have to do any of these things unless they very much felt like it. The artsy-craftsy boutique closed after four months, and the receptionist stopped receptioning when her husband arranged for a summer in Europe. I did what I did because somehow I hadn't been clever enough to remarry, this time snaring a man who would support me. If I thought of Jim O'Donnell's friend as Poor Ilona, at family conferences I was Poor Martine.

But this was not Alicia's version of my life; hers was titillating—to her, and the day she called I wasn't really in the mood for her questions about Andy Lang. I had taken Andy to a press party some weeks before and we had met Alicia and Larry O'Malley there. Larry is a public relations man, and we often found ourselves sipping free liquor at the same parties.

I had introduced Andy to the O'Malleys, and ever since I'd been doing my best to avoid having long conversations with Alicia. Alicia is one of those marvelous people who never watches television. She considers it a terrible waste of time. Nor does she ever read a book. Alicia, whenever she has a free second, is on the telephone talking to one or another of a large network of friends and describing in minute detail who did what to whom, where and why.

Now it was my turn.

"Martine, ever since we met you at the Mayor's press party I've been dying to talk to you."

"Here I am."

"Who was that terrific guy we saw you with?"

"Which terrific guy?"

"You know. He's tall, with dark wavy hair, and a great smile."

I could have gotten away with saying he was a business associate, but I didn't feel like bothering.

"He's just a friend, Alicia, that's all. A friend."

Alicia giggled. "Is he married?"

"Why do you ask?"

"Just curious."

"Yes, he's married."

Alicia was breathless. "I told Larry. That's just what I told him! I said, 'I bet he's married.' Martine, are you serious about him? What's happening?"

I couldn't help it. I retreated. It was just easier.

"Alicia, he's just a business associate. I have a million of them. I may be doing some free-lance copywriting for his ad agency. That's all."

"Oh."

Alicia was disappointed. Her life was moral, but her fantasies were not. She would have loved hearing about my affair, and she would never have uttered a critical word. I would be doing what she yearned to do. She would also have loved hearing what had happened with Andy, Jim, and Poor Ilona, but I wasn't in the mood for her sympathy.

"How's Larry?" I asked. "And the kids?"

"Fine. Everyone's fine. We're giving a party a week from Saturday. Can you come?"

"Sure," I answered. "I'll be there."

"Would you like to bring someone? I mean, if there's anyone you'd like to bring, I'd be more than happy—"

"Fine," I said, "I'll ask Dee Dee. If she's not busy I'm sure she'd love to come."

Alicia and Dee Dee despised each other.

"Oh, I didn't mean . . . of course, Dee Dee is welcome."

"Maybe it would be best if I came by myself," I said, pretending to give the matter a great deal of thought. "That is, if you don't think I'll be *de trop*, a single woman."

"No, not at all, that'll be fine." I could hear the relief in Alicia's voice when she realized I wouldn't be bringing Dee Dee. "*De trop*, Martine, that's so silly, coming from you. We'll see you next Saturday, then, around eight?"

"Eight sounds fine. Thanks, Alicia. I'm looking forward to it."

After I hung up I wondered why I had agreed to go. I hated Alicia and Larry's parties. A party like theirs probably preceded Noah's Ark and the flood. Everybody arrived two-by-two. The women went off to one side of the room to discuss children in various stages of development: everything from toilet training to the high cost of private prep school. And the men went off to discuss business.

Not even my mother used her "if you don't go, you won't know" line when it came to Alicia and Larry's parties. She was ready to admit up front that she didn't believe it possible that I could ever meet anyone interesting at the O'Malleys'.

"They never have anyone there," she had said when I had described a typical O'Malley party.

"They have about twenty people," I had said.

"All *petit bourgeois*."

"Is that worse than *haut bourgeois*?"

"Much."

My mother was truly angry when I told her that Alicia had asked about Andy and then given her reason for asking as curiosity.

"She was 'just curious!' *Curious*—what kind of word

131

is that to use to a friend? Not interest, not concerned, *curious*!''

''Mom, she didn't mean anything terrible. *Curious* is not a bad word. It probably means something different in French.''

''Curious is curious, in English as in French. It's a cold, uncaring word. Please don't teach me English, Martine.''

And now I was committed to a Saturday night party at the O'Malleys.

If we were lucky, Larry and I could talk to each other. For some reason, Larry rarely brought anyone home from his office. The men at his house were the husbands of Alicia's friends, the ''girls'' she met in the neighborhood, the playground, the shops, at PTA meetings. Larry had as much in common with the husbands as I had with the wives. I had decided that Larry's life was so centered on Alicia and the kids that he didn't care about making friends among the people he worked with. Whatever his reason, it made for pretty dull parties.

Never mind, I was committed for a week from Saturday night, and I would get through it by telling myself that it was just one evening. But before that, I had to decide about Andy. Not that there was that much to decide. What difference did it make if we parted in the middle of the summer or at the end of it? We were going to part, that much was sure. Why not get it over with?

''Martine?'' Andy's call came after Alicia's. ''Look, I don't know what's wrong, but can we get together tonight and talk?''

''Of course.'' Now that my decision had been made

132

I did not feel as badly as I thought I would. I felt relieved.

"At the apartment," he was asking, "or—"

"Let's meet out. Any place but the Carlyle."

"How about the cocktail lounge at the U.N. Plaza Hotel? That's a nice, neutral corner."

Andy sounded cheerful enough, and that made me think that he had come to the same decision I had reached. "It was great fun, but it was just one of those things."

"That sounds fine," I agreed, and we said we'd meet at six o'clock.

CHAPTER XVII

Andy

Martine and I were going to meet for drinks at the U.N. Plaza Hotel bar. It's not my favorite bar, too many mirrors and the decor a little too cold. But it was comfortable and it was close to Martine's apartment. I was pleased we were meeting, but a little uneasy that it wasn't going to be at Martine's apartment. My unease stayed with me all day, and I got to the bar a little early. Martine arrived promptly carrying a bulging manila envelope. We kissed each other lightly and I ordered drinks.

"Baby, I'm sorry about last night. Jim's not important enough to come between us. I won't let it happen again."

"That's all right, you couldn't help it. Jim's your friend. I got upset last night and I'm sorry, too. Here." She extended the manila envelope for me to take.

Another present? A peace offering? I unwrapped the package and inside was the robe she had given me.

"What's this all about?"

"I'm sorry, Andy. It just won't work. I mean, we won't. You're a wonderful man and we've been wonderful together, but you're a married man with two children you love. It's just too painful, in spite of all the fun we've had. So that's it. It's time to say good bye."

"Martine, you can't end it like this. I love you—you know that. And you love me, I know that. You've told me that, and shown me that, too many times. I can't end because of a stupid episode like last night. Goddamn that Jim."

"It wasn't just Jim. He only reminded me that you have a family. We have to sneak around to keep from being seen. It's been a lovely summer, but what happens when it's over and your wife and girls come home? Will I see you one night a week when you're supposed to be out with the boys?"

Her arguments were strong and her position adamant. I couldn't tell her I would run off and leave my wife and kids and marry her.

It was easier to stay the way we were. I couldn't face the explanations I would have to make to my kids, my family. Besides. I had known plenty of men who had gotten divorced, and the process had left them exhausted and drained emotionally, physically, and financially.

Divorce was commonplace enough and new laws had supposedly made it easier. But it was never easy for the people involved. I just couldn't handle it.

As we left the bar I asked if I could walk her home

and she agreed. "Good idea. You can pick up the rest of your clothes and things."

We walked glumly down the street with the package under my arm. I wanted to find a trash basket and throw it away, but I couldn't. As we walked up First Avenue I saw a florist shop that had a large, artificial paper rose about five feet high in the window. It was so outsized and grotesque it was funny. I asked Martine to wait while I went inside the store and I tried to buy it. It wasn't really for sale, the florist explained, it was a display for the store. For enough money I persuaded him to let me have it. I had him wrap it as an ordinary bouquet and I enclosed a card. She was waiting outside and I presented her with the flower.

Martine enjoyed the exaggerated rose as much as I did. Gleefully she unwrapped the package, found the card, and read it aloud. "One perfect rose that will never die. Like my love for you."

She started to sob then and came into my arms, still sobbing. It wasn't over.

CHAPTER XVIII

Martine

After I had told Andy I would meet him for a drink at the U.N. Plaza Hotel I bustled about as though what I was doing was of the greatest importance. I plucked Andy's robe from the closet. My hands were shaking, and I realized I was so furious I could hardly breathe. But that made it easier. I folded the robe, tucked it neatly into a manila clasp envelope and left the apartment. I walked part of the way, hoping the exercise would calm me, but I took a cab for the last ten blocks because I was breathing hard and choking on tears.

I should have taken a Miltown, but I was glad I hadn't. I didn't want Andy to see some calm zombie. I wanted him to see me as I really was. I wanted him to know how he had made me feel.

The cocktail lounge at the U.N. Plaza Hotel really is a neutral corner. It is cold and elegant, and the abundance of lights against the mirrored walls and glass ceilings make me unsure as to whether I'm viewing a reflected image or seeing deep into another room.

"Martine." Andy's smile was warm and sweet, and he moved so quickly towards me that his martini slopped over on the highly polished tabletop. "God, I'm glad to see you."

I didn't say anything. I couldn't, my chest felt so tight. He kissed me and I kissed him back. Why not? It was the last time.

"Martine." He said that a few times, and then, "I've missed you. One night without you. I didn't know how it would be. I really missed you."

I knew what he meant. Just one night apart. I hadn't known, either, not until I sat beside him, just how very much I had missed him. But I didn't want him to know that I knew—and felt—the way he did. When in doubt, be amusing. And that's what I was. I told him about something funny that had happened to me and Dee Dee six months ago, only I pretended that it had happened the day before.

He laughed and looked happy, and I knew it wasn't just because of my story. It was because he thought everything was all right between the two of us and that whatever had bothered foolish Martine was bothering her no longer.

"Would you like to have dinner here," he asked, "or shall we go elsewhere?"

"Let's go for a walk," I said. "We can decide about dinner later."

"All right." He called for a check. "Oh, Martine," Andy put his arm about me, and tried to draw me closer, "Martine, you don't know—"

"Andy, wait," I pulled away from him, and I held

140

the manila envelope out to him. "Here. This is for you."

I was hoping he wouldn't grin like a kid getting a present; he had once told me that I was the only one ever to give him a gift, and when I remembered that I almost pulled the envelope back. But something about the way I looked, I guess, told him this was not about to be a happy surprise.

He opened the envelope, reached in, and saw his robe. Andy pushed the robe back into the envelope and closed the clasp. He held the envelope out to me.

"Take it back, Martine."

I shook my head.

"Please. Take it back. It's not over. Not yet."

"Yes it is," I said. "There's no reason for it not to be over."

"All because of what happened at the Carlyle? Because of that idiot Jim?"

"No. That started it, but that's not why."

"Then why?"

"Because you're a married man with two children, and you're going to stay a married man with two children, and I'm not going to turn into a Poor Ilona waiting for something that can't happen."

Andy clutched the envelope to him. "Let's walk."

We left the hotel and walked up First Avenue slowly.

"I love you, Martine."

"No."

"Yes, I do."

I thought, if you think this is love, you don't know what love is. I had love with Davy, but I can't teach it to you. Poor Andy. He must have thought he was in love with his wife when he married her, but if you've

141

never had love as a child, how do you know what love is? I felt sorry for him, but it was too late. It wasn't up to me to teach him something I had learned about as a child.

"It doesn't matter," I said.

"If that doesn't matter, then you tell me what in God's name does."

"Wives matter," I said. "And children matter. You know that better than I."

Andy took a deep breath. "Yes, I do know, but why can't we wait? Why do we have to say goodbye now? It's not time."

"The longer we wait, the harder it will be." How much harder could it be? I wondered.

We continued walking, and I tried to concentrate on the store windows. The neighborhood deli, the Viennese pastry shop, the Chinese laundry, the antique boutique.

"Wait." Andy pulled on my arm, making me stop in front of a florist. "I have to get you one of those."

He pointed to something in the window, but I didn't really know what he was pointing to until he came out of the store carrying the biggest, grandest, craziest, reddest paper rose I had ever seen. The stem was four feet long, and each petal was the size of my palm. He held the flower before him, and I could just make out his eyes above the petals.

"Here," he said, holding that absurd flower out to me, "I want you to have this, Martine. It's one perfect rose."

I took the flower and I started to laugh, and then I started to cry.

"Martine," Andy held the manila envelope out to me, "please take this back, please."

I took the manila envelope, and Andy reached for me, and the paper flower was pressed between us.

"Please," I tried to pull back, "you're crushing my rose."

He let me go, and I carried the paper rose before me as we walked back to my apartment.

CHAPTER XIX

Andy

Labor Day came and the summer was over. It was time for Janet and the kids to come home and for all of us to resume our normal lives. The kids would be enrolled in nursery school and my traveling to Fire Island on weekends was over.

But what about my idyll with Martine? Was that over too? There was no question that I loved her in a way I didn't love Janet now, and never remembered loving Janet, not even in the early days.

There were no thoughts in my head I would stop seeing Martine. I couldn't spend nights with her any more, nor could I see her every evening during the week as I had been doing. We would have to be even more circumspect in our choice of public meeting places because Janet's friends were also back from their vacations on Fire Island. I felt we would manage somehow.

I saw Martine at irregular times whenever I could manufacture an excuse. Often it was just for cocktails or lunch. To me, those times were never enough. Whenever we were able to sleep together it was almost like an explosion, a reunion of two lovers having been parted for much longer than just a few days.

Janet and I renewed our normal city routine. I would go to work in the morning. Janet expected me to have dinner with the children. She believed it was psychologically necessary for children to have dinner with both parents every night. I loved my kids, but I didn't like having my schedule determined by them.

I also hated having dinner at six. I almost always had a business lunch with a client, associate, or vendor, and I wasn't hungry when I got home. I liked a late dinner, leisurely, civilized, relaxed, European. Instead of eating with my kids, I'd keep them company at the table and have my dinner later.

But if I was going to be later than six, I'd have to call and explain by no later than four that afternoon, or there would be a scene with Janet.

One day a client arrived unexpectedly and announced that we had a crisis that demanded the agency's immediate attention. We worked through lunch and the entire afternoon. At about six-thirty he said he was hungry and asked if we could have dinner at a nearby restaurant and continue working. Immediately after dinner we went back to my office. The meeting ended about nine, the crisis resolved, the account saved for the agency. The client went to catch a plane and I went home. I'd never called Janet to tell her I would be late, but I hadn't expected to have dinner with the client, either.

146

I let myself into the apartment to be greeted by a furious Janet.

"Where the hell have you been?"

"Working. The client came to the office unexpectedly this morning and we've been working until fifteen minutes ago."

"Is that so? I've cooked a roast leg of lamb. The kids were waiting for you. I had to feed them myself, bathe them myself, and put them to bed myself. Why didn't you call? How long does it take to call? Couldn't you just pick up the phone? Now you're going to tell me you're not hungry because you've had dinner with your client. After I slaved all afternoon making your favorite roast."

"No, I didn't have dinner. He had to catch a plane—that's why we worked right through. I haven't eaten."

I sat down with Janet opposite me. She placed the leg of lamb platter in front of me to carve. Lamb is one of my favorite dishes, but I carved myself the thinnest slices possible, and I gave Janet thicker pieces.

I then began to cut the meat on my plate, and I remembered my mother saying, "Chew each piece nine times before you swallow." I counted every chew. Janet was finished before I was and left the table.

I continued living my double life with increasing strain. I shared a bed with Janet every night, and I didn't want to. On weekends, from Friday evening to Monday morning, the kids were entirely mine. That was the arrangement Janet worked out. That way I could spend more time with the children, she said—it was only fair. We should divide all work connected with the children exactly in half. She had it figured out to the hour, including the hours the girls spent in nurery school, with the babysitter, and with the cleaninwoman who came in once a week.

Weekends gave Janet her space. She used it to go exercise class, visit museums, and sleep late.

I came home later than usual several evenings a weejust so I could see Martine for an hour or so. I had see her, touch her. I would tell Janet I was havindinner with a client or my boss, and I would spend thentire evening with Martine at her apartment. Thcreated a problem, too, because my clients would arive in town unexpectedly from time to time, and the would insist that I join them for dinner.

Janet began asking me more detailed questions abouwhy I was getting home so late. I invented elaboratstories to explain my late evenings.

One evening over dinner Janet said, "I saw JudSaylor this afternoon. We went to the new Matisse ehibit at the Modern. She told me she saw you at I Cygne with a very attractive girl. Who was she?"

This is it, I thought. I continued eating with my eyon the plate, seemingly unconcerned about the quetion.

"Joanne Benson," I said, "one of the people on thsoup account. They're changing the product formuland we're working out a joint advertising and publrelations program."

"You eat lunch at fancy French restaurants," Jancommented, "and I eat tuna salad sandwiches with thkids."

"Why didn't you have lunch with Judy?"

"The babysitter called to say she was coming a littlater today."

There was nothing I could say to that, and we ate the rest of our dinner in silence. Janet went off to bed immediately after, and I put the dishes in the dishwasher and got the girls to bed.

My affair with Martine was beginning to affect my nerves and my health. I would find myself being snappish with everybody. I had trouble sleeping. Janet complained about my grinding my teeth in the middle of the night. She asked me to stop because it woke her. I was always looking over my shoulder when I was with Martine, afraid of being seen. It got so I looked at people suspiciously even when I wasn't with Martine. Something had to be done. I couldn't go on this way much longer.

I'm not a Catholic, but when it came to marriage I felt like one. Kids, family disapproval, money problems, habit—all that was enough for me to want to stay married.

"Janet," I said one evening, after the kids were in bed, "I've got an idea. Let's go away for the weekend. Just the two of us. We'll drive to the country, find a small inn where no one can reach us. What do you say?"

"What about the kids?"

"We'll leave them with your sister. She's crazy about them, and they like her. They can play with her kids—they get along fine. It'll be like old times—just the two of us. How about it?"

"I don't like leaving the girls, especially Diane. I read about it in the *Times*. Some famous child psychologist said that leaving a child under five overnight, or for a few days, is traumatic. He said it was like death. And Diane's only four."

I pleaded. "Many people leave their children for a night or a week all the time and the children don't turn schizophrenic or paranoid or anything. Look at Dot, look at Pearl, look at Jane. They go away for vacations without their kids, and their kids don't chew their pillows, turn blue, or starve. Besides, let's think of us. We haven't been alone for a single night since Barbara was born.

"Think of it this way. No cooking, washing, cleaning, wiping noses, or whispering when we make love for two whole days. We'll just indulge each other. And as for the kids, it's just for two days—two days, they'll be fine. Please, we owe it to ourselves."

She finally said, "All right. But only if my sister agrees to take the girls."

Gratefully I got up and tried to take her in my arms and give her a kiss.

"Not now," she said. "The girls are still awake. They'll hear us. Maybe later."

Nevertheless I had won. It could work. It would work. I was determined. I'd resurrect our early passion. I made mental plans for the weekend and they all revolved around romance with Janet. I wanted an untroubled life.

Martine was lovely, kind, generous. Fabulous in bed. It must be true about the French. Everything about her was erotic and shamelessly so. But she wasn't my wife, and she wasn't the mother of my two kids.

Martine wasn't real. She was my fantasy, and a grown man should know the difference between fantasy and reality. The weekend with Janet would put my world back into proper perspective.

The weekend was an unqualified and complete di

aster. First we took the children to my sister-in-law's house; she was glad to have them stay with her. Then off we drove to Mystic, Connecticut. We stayed in nearby New London at a beautiful old hotel overlooking Long Island Sound. It was small, luxurious, a throwback to a more leisurely time.

Over dinner, I gave Janet a pearl necklace. The pearls were small but beautifully matched. I had spent several lunch hours shopping for them. She smiled, and let me help her put them on. We each had two drinks, and I ordered a good bottle of Pommard. I tried to talk about us, but Janet kept bringing the conversation around to schools for the kids and redecorating the apartment.

We went back to our room which overlooked the Sound.

"Janet," I said, "look at the lights over the water."

"I can't look at anything," she murmured. "Those drinks—that wine. I've got to lie down."

And with that, Janet fell asleep.

I was up early next morning, and I took a walk. There was a beautiful marina nearby with a variety of sailboats. Knowing how Janet liked boats, I went back to the hotel and woke her, planning to take her to the marina after breakfast.

Right after breakfast Janet called her sister, who said, "Don't hurry back, your kids and my kids are having a great time."

I had the feeling that Janet was disappointed, but she was willing to walk over to the marina. As we were standing on the dock we saw a good-sized sailboat in the distance.

"Look at the way that boat's being handled," Jane said. "Terrific!"

The boat came closer, and we saw the man who was sailing her bring the boat neatly to a mooring. He threw a rope to the dock, jumped out of the boat, and secured the sailboat. The guy looked good. White ducks, blue striped jersey, and a captain's hat tilted over one eye. He started walking towards us, and heard a little gasp from Janet.

The man saw her at the same moment. He hesitated, and then he raised his hand in a half-wave. Janet waved back, and the man walked towards us.

"Janet," he said, "hi."

"Hi, Dick," Janet said, and she introduced me to Dick Templeton.

We shook hands, and I stood there politely listening to the two of them make small talk. There he was, my wife's ex-lover. Janet had told me about him, and had asked her when I proposed if she was hesitating because she was carrying a torch for another man.

"No torch," she had said then, "I'm just afraid of being hurt again."

Looking at her now—eight years later—I knew she hadn't told the truth then. The way they were looking at each other, there was something still smoldering between them.

They said goodbye.

"It was great seeing you, Janet."

"Great seeing you, too, Dick."

It was so great for the two of them that they forgot I was standing there. Dick Templeton, the man Janet should have married. How the hell had our lives become so scrambled?

Janet and I wandered around Mystic for the rest of the day, visiting the whaling museum and the old sailing ships, but neither of us noticed much of what we were looking at.

We didn't talk much that night at supper. Can you imagine an entire dinner deliberately not talking about something? We didn't talk about Dick, but he was right there with us at the table.

In bed that night Janet was tired, had a headache, just couldn't—maybe tomorrow—and escaped into sleep. We left New London early next day, and when we got to Janet's sister's house Diane and Barbara greeted us with:

"What did you bring me?"

Then they went back to playing with their cousins.

It was a view into the future. I could see what my kids—all kids—are like once they're grown. This is what my parents said when they complained about me and my brother. We didn't pay enough attention to them and saw them only on holidays or at family parties. I imagined my daughters grown and living their own lives. There would be dutifull calls and family dinners at Thanksgiving and Christmas. And me alone with Janet.

I had been brought up to believe that life consisted of responsibility, obligation, and duty. Love was not a necessary part of life, according to my parents, though it was nice in the movies.

We collected the kids, put them in the car, and drove back to the city. Janet talked happily with Diane and Barbara. Janet and I had nothing to say to each other.

CHAPTER XX

Martine

Waiting for that summer to end was terrible. I wanted it to end because I hate waiting for disasters. Better to get them over with.

I remember when Davy was sick, and a few years later my father became ill. I knew each was going to die, and during their last few days I wanted them dead.

remember listening to the hoarse rasping sound that came from my father's throat and chest as he tried desperately to breathe, and I remember wanting him to die, hoping he would die as I slept and he slept.

Of course, the next day because of my own guilt and fear I was in a frenzy to have him live—if only for a few hours—and it was my insistence that made the doctor give him an injection that brought him screaming from his comatose state.

Now I was presiding over the last few days of a dying

affair, and I wanted that to end, too. Let it be soon let it be quick, please let's cut the pain short.

I once tried to explain my reaction to this sort of pain to my cousin Katy. I had shocked her by saying "Pain is so boring; waiting for someone to die. That kind of pain fills me with ennui."

"Boring. Is that all you can call it?"

I could not explain, just as I could not explain to Andy that it would be best to say goodbye before the last minute arrived. After that day when I tried to give Andy his robe, and he brought me that gigantic blooming paper rose, it was clear that we were going to spend the rest of the summer together. Except for Andy's weekends on Fire Island. Weekends which he cut as short as he dared, taking an earlier ferry away from the island with each consecutive Sunday.

"Doesn't Janet say anything?"

"I don't think she cares," he said.

"If she doesn't care and you don't care, why do you stay together?"

That brought on a litany about family. He told me about a family that emphasized duty rather than love, preached a harsh religion without ever once tempering it with God's mercy. A family that sacrificed everything for children and believed that the children should continue that sacrifice when they had children of their own. The idea of pleasure was anathema in Andy's childhood.

"My mother once said to me in real anger, 'All you think about is having fun,'" Andy said.

"And my mother still says, 'If you're feeling down or depressed, give a party.'"

We stared at each other.

156

"That's why you are the way you are," Andy said. "But you, I would have thought you would have anted to get away from your family, marry someone ompletely different."

"I thought I did marry someone completely differ- nt," Andy said. "I thought Janet was the exact op- osite of my mother. It turns out she's exactly the ame."

That was the middle of August. And soon it was the nd of August and that strange holiday, Labor Day, was bout to arrive. And then it was Thursday night. Our st Thursday night. Our last night together. I mar- eted for all our favorites. As my mother said, when epressed, give a party, and I decided on a party for he two of us, with all our special foods. There was moked Scotch salmon, a bounty of sliced raw onions, heeses, dense and delicious breads, and fine cham- agne to be drunk straight by me or combined with a hot of vodka for Andy's French 75s.

We ate in bed on trays in front of the television set. forgot to say how enchanted Andy was when he dis- overed that I loved television.

"Janet almost never watches television," he told me. 'she calls it the boob tube."

We were like two children coming to the end of a vonderful, childish romp, and I decided that our party, ist like any good children's party, should have two esserts, ice cream and cake. I concocted Andy's fa- orite, his hot fudge ice cream sundae, for which I vhipped the cream, and a truly chocolate cake. The quares of chocolate cake were paved with chocolate lavored whipped cream and topped with chocolate ic- ng.

"Can't get more chocolate than that," I said.

Andy laughed and dug a spoon into the ice cream, a fork into the cake. But he stopped eating after a few bites, and so did I. I put away the fish, the cheese, the bread, and the cake, but I brought another bottle of champagne to the bedroom.

"I'll call you on Tuesday," Andy said.

"Yes."

"As soon as I get to my office. First thing in the morning."

I put the champagne glass down carefully and buried my face in a pillow.

"Martine? Are you all right? Can you breathe?"

I nodded my head. I could breathe, but I didn't really know if I wanted to.

Andy left early the next morning, and that left me with a whole wonderful weekend all to myself. I had made no plans, telling myself that this was the perfect time to catch up on two articles that were both due within a few weeks. Wonderful idea. Except that one article was for *Bride's Magazine*, titled "Disappointments—How to Avoid Them—How to Live With Them." This was one of a series of lacily written pieces that I was doing on how brides could cope. The readers loved them, and one of the editors named them, "Martine's geisha pieces." That was certainly my geisha summer.

Never did I feel less like writing about disappointments, so I put that one aside and tackled another minor masterpiece for a general-interest woman's magazine on camping out with the family. Fascinating, I realized after staring at the typewriter that this was not the weekend to work. I called Dee Dee, who was

158

in an equally happy state about a theme song she was attempting to write for a Twentieth Century-Fox spy movie.

I went over to Dee Dee's apartment, and after a quick consultation she sent out for a container of iced coffee for me and a container of iced tea for herself.

I had once suggested to Dee Dee that it just might be possible to boil some water for tea or coffee in her kitchen, but she had looked so horrified I had never mentioned it again.

"I'm an artist," she had said. "I don't cook. That's a terrible waste of creative energy. I'll never understand why you do so much cooking, Martine."

"I've got creative energy to burn."

"No one has," she said.

The coffee and tea arrived in elegant paper containers, and we sipped.

"Delicious," I said.

"So?" Dee Dee made slurping noises through her straw.

"So what?"

"Has he gone back to the Virgin Mother and Children?"

"What are you talking about, Dee Dee?"

"Some guy I knew in Rome took me to this museum once and showed me this great oil painting. At least he said it was great. It was the Madonna with the infant Jesus. I realized that's what's wrong with a lot of the guys we know. They see their wives as the Madonnas and their kids as little Jesus Christs. They forget their wives are not Virgin Marys and for them to get pregnant they had to spread their legs just like the rest of us."

159

"Dee Dee, enough."

"Okay, I was just thinking."

"How's the new song coming?"

"Wonderful. I'm thinking of rhyming moon with June. How's your article for Condé Nast coming?"

"Just as wonderful as your song."

"That's what I figured. Listen, I may have to go out to the coast for a few weeks—how about coming with me?"

"I hate the coast."

"Lots of TV work out there. I could introduce you. A lot more money than you're making here."

"I told you, I hate the coast, I hate the people. You can't walk into a restaurant without everyone trying to figure out who you are, what you do, who you're sleeping with."

Dee Dee shrugged, "So don't eat out. They deliver great iced coffee there, too."

"It's not for me."

"It's because you don't want to leave town, because of that guy."

"That has nothing to do with it."

"Don't tell me. I know the signs. Listen, Martine, believe me, he'll never leave that wife, no matter how bitchy she is, not while she has those kids. Remember the Virgin Mary. Did Joseph leave her flat? And he must have wondered at some time about that kid."

"Dee Dee, quit it!"

"Okay, I'm just saying it for your own good. I didn't make up the story. It's as old as the Bible."

I didn't say anything, and Dee Dee realized I'd had enough.

160

"You want to eat out," she asked, "or should I send out for a pizza?"

I didn't want to eat, but I couldn't face the sight of another paper plate or container.

"Out," I said.

And out we went.

CHAPTER XXI

Martine

With Andy at home with Janet and the children, I decided to take another look at Peregrine. He had just returned from the Midwest and West where he had been gathering material for an article on Americans he was writing for an English magazine.

"Another article on how Americans live," I had said when he had told me of the assignment. "There's been a million of them."

"Not like mine. Mine will be the definitive one. It will incorporate my point of view."

Did I also mention that Peregrine was pompous? But the summer had mellowed my feelings towards him. I was willing to overlook the stuffiness because he was there and because he had come back to New York and me, while Andy had left me for Janet.

"How was your summer?" Peregrine asked the first night he came over. "What have you been doing?"

I hesitated, unsure as to how I should answer that question. But Peregrine took me off the hook.

"Did you get a lot of work done? Finish those nonsense pieces for that bridal magazine? How's the book coming?"

I answered his questions gratefully: yes, the magazine articles were done; no, I hadn't written a line for a novel I was trying to do; and from there I plunged in to all the gossipy bits about the people we both knew in the publishing business. He laughed when I told him about my weekend with Corey and his shoplifting girlfriend, and I gave him the latest on the tall, blonde editor-in-chief of a general interest magazine we both wrote for.

"Who's she sleeping with these days?" Peregrine asked me.

"How would I know?"

"Don't you have dinner with her from time to time? I know the two of you do that disgusting bit of shopping together like a couple of addled schoolgirls."

"It's fun being an addled schoolgirl from time to time," I said, "and she's fun to be with, too, but I don't really ask her who she's sleeping with."

"Never mind," Peregrine said. "I'll just read the next few issues of her magazine. She makes it with most of the male contributors."

"Oh, I don't know."

"I do," Peregrine said, and downed his scotch and water, no ice, please.

Of course. Peregrine had been a frequent contributor to the magazine, writing fascinating articles on the real background of World War I, the primitive tribesmen of the South Pacific, and why singles bars were

164

an American phenomenon. For some reason I had never really understood until that very moment, the tall blonde editor had stopped giving Peregrine assignments. I was glad that Corey was willing to settle for my picking up an occasional lunch check.

"Oh," I said.

Peregrine held his glass out to me. "May I have another drink? What else have you been doing this summer? How's Dee Dee? Have you been seeing anyone special?"

The question was casual, but I knew Peregrine. He had his own defenses. If I said yes, he would go back to talking about the publishing business. If I said no, it would give him the opening to talk about us.

Why should I say yes? If Andy had been someone special, it would have lasted past the summer. And at the moment I hurt from the seeming ease with which he had moved back to his wife and children. Why tell Peregrine about him at all? I didn't ask him about the girls he had met in Texas, or the ones who had fallen for his English accent in Ohio.

"No," I answered. "No one special."

Peregrine allowed himself to look a little pleased, but then he surprised me by talking business again.

"My agent tells me that I may be offered a very big contract quite soon," he said.

"What kind of contract? To do what?"

"A series of travel books. It would mean moving to Europe for a year or two. Traveling about, doing really in-depth books for people who want more than the ordinary Cook's tour."

"How's the money?"

165

"A decent advance. A good percentage of the royalties, and a fair amount for expenses."

"Good for you, Peregrine," I said, and I meant it. Peregrine was one of the few free-lance writers around who wouldn't cut another writer's throat to get ahead. And getting to live in Europe at a publisher's expenses, that was a dream both Peregrine and I shared, and it was nice that it had come true for one of us. "I'm happy for you," I said, and I genuinely was.

"How about you, Martine? Wouldn't you like to live in Europe for a while?"

"Of course. And maybe some day I'll get lucky too."

"Come with me. I'll be leaving in about six weeks. We could get married. Or not. Whichever you prefer."

Peregrine's proposal was so indifferent, so casual, I wasn't sure I had understood him.

"Did you say . . . Are you asking me to marry you, Peregrine?"

"Yes," he brushed that bit of un-Peregrine-like sentimentality aside, "and I'm asking you to come to Europe with me. It's just possible we could collaborate on the travel books. Or perhaps you could get an advance on your novel. Write it in Europe. If not, I'm sure you could line up some magazine assignments to do abroad. What brides are worrying about in Paris, or how to avoid disappointments in Rome, that sort of thing."

I laughed, "It's not that bad, Peregrine."

"Yes it is. You keep saying you want to write something serious, and you keep putting it off. Either do it or forget it, Martine."

166

He was right, of course. I felt comfortable with Peregrine in a way that I had never felt with Andy. He understood my work because we were both doing the same thing, grinding out trivia while promising ourselves to do something more important someday.

"It's the money," I said, as I had said to him, and to myself, a million times before. "I need time, and that means money, to sit down and write a good book."

Peregrine looked about. He looked at my silk drapes, my Thaibok-silk-covered couches, my hand-woven rug from Portugal, and my gold-threaded caftan from Saks.

"You could have money," he said, "If you didn't spend it so foolishly."

"Peregrine—"

"All right, forget it."

Neither one of us was in the mood for repetition of the argument we had many times before, the argument about the way I spent my hard-earned money. Peregrine lectured me frequently on my spendthrift habits. Phrases such as "an iron ration" and "you should put your money into interest-bearing shares" were often repeated. I knew that Peregrine lived frugally; cheaply was the way my mother put it.

But I also knew that Peregrine was right. Free-lance writers, unless born to wealth, have nothing to fall back on. No unemployment insurance, no medical plan unless they pay for it themselves. Editors change, and new editors come to magazines and publishing companies with their own stables of pets. And even if editors remained, fashions changed, as a fickle public looked for more titillating or more serious or more angry or sweeter pieces.

Peregrine had money saved against those months

when no one would give him an assignment. In addition, he was switching from articles to books, something he had urged me to do for months. Smart practical Peregrine. Why would someone as practical as Peregrine want to marry me?

"Peregrine, are you in love with me?"

"What? Oh, do stop that, Martine."

"But Peregrine, you just asked me to marry you. You did, didn't you? Why did you, if you don't love me?"

"I suppose I do love you, Martine, but I don't see that it's anything we have to talk about. Besides, there are more important things than love. We get along. We're in the same business. We like the same things, have many of the same tastes. I think we'd last a lot longer than people who marry because of all that romantic nonsense."

That made me think of Andy again. Ours had been lovely, childlike, romantic nonsense. And how long had it lasted? One brief summer. Maybe Peregrine was right. He certainly was giving me a convenient way out. I could just hear myself saying it all to Andy when, or if, he called again.

"Andy? Good to talk to you again, but I am in a rush. I have so much to do. I'm going to Europe in six weeks. Yes, Paris first. No, not alone. I'm getting married."

It was a Steig dream of glory, a child's fantasy of getting even, and it was what was in my mind when I went to bed with Peregrine that night. The trouble was that you can't be marvelous with one man in bed if you're busy thinking about another.

That was one trouble; here are some of the others:

168

Peregrine was so satisfied with the way things went in my bedroom that he didn't even know that I wasn't. He was so smug about his orgasm, and so unaware that I never had one, that I could have hit him.

I kept comparing. Everything. The way Peregrine's body didn't make me feel, the way Andy's had. Peregrine's slim shoulders to Andy's broad ones. Peregrine's body, I suddenly realized, looked better in clothing than nude. Peregrine was so smug about his penis, he was so proud of what it had accomplished, he almost crooned to it. (My God, there still are men out there who believe the myth of penis envy.)

I wanted Peregrine to go home. I had never wanted Andy to leave. But I lay in bed, my shoulder, hip, and thigh touching Peregrine's shoulder, hip, and thigh, and I hoped that he wouldn't want to stay the night. I hadn't felt a thing during our lovemaking, maybe not completely Peregrine's fault, but that not-feeling made me want desperately to be alone. I was lonely with Peregrine; I would be less lonely with him gone.

Luckily, Peregrine was practical as always. He had proposed to me, sealed the bargain by a technically correct fucking, and now he had to go home because he had an early morning meeting with his agent, and if he didn't leave now he'd have to leave very early to change his clothes, pick up his manuscript, and so on.

As I watched Peregrine dress I had the feeling that he might want to be alone just as much as I did. I have a friend, twice divorced, who says that the only way she would consider remarrying is if she and the man could keep separate apartments, meeting every evening at cocktail time. I thought of introducing her to Peregrine. Some people are not meant to live with others;

I wondered if Peregrine realized he might be one of them. But, no, Peregrine was as self-satisfied with his clothes on as with them off.

"I'll call tomorrow," he said at my door. "And we'll make plans."

I didn't have the guts to tell him the truth. "Yes Peregrine."

It would be easier to tell him over the phone. Meanwhile, it was almost midnight, and after I showered, I changed my mind about wanting to be alone. If Peregrine hadn't proposed and we hadn't gone to bed, he would have been the one I would have called to see if he wanted to go out for a drink or to see the midnight *Rocky Horror Show*. Damn, not only had Peregrine fucked me, in both the literal and pejorative sense, but he had also fucked up our friendship—in the pejorative sense alone.

I called Dee Dee and got her answering machine. Sometimes Dee Dee is prescient. "Whoever you are," her metallic recording said, "call me tomorrow. Unless it's Martine. Martine, if you call between twelve and one, meet me at the Sign of the Dove. I'll be there till one with two guys from Twentieth-Century Fox."

That's just what I needed, to go to the Sign of the Dove—a restaurant I hated—with two of Dee Dee's slickers, the kind of men I hated. Ridiculous. I'd be better off staying in bed. First, I'd make myself some frozen blintzes that I had stashed in the freezer. I'd fry them in a ton of butter and eat them in bed while watching an old movie on TV. But the idea of doing the warm and familiar depressed me even further. Besides, my mother always said that if you don't go, you won't know. Maybe Dee Dee had my Prince Charm-

170

ing with her, the man I was waiting for, a combination of my two old movie favorites: Cary Grant and Fred Astaire, without a wife and children. After all, not everyone in the movie business had to be a mean, destructive, male chauvinist son-of-a-bitch. And it was in this open-minded manner that I dressed, left my house, hailed a cab and went over to the Sign of the Dove.

Dee Dee was pleased to see me, but she wasn't surprised.

"Nobody can spend a whole night with an Englishman," she said. "I tried it once and almost died of the cold."

The Twentieth-Century Fox men laughed, though they didn't know what they were laughing at. They just wanted a tumble in bed and figured that laughing at what the girls said would give them a better chance.

"We went to the theater tonight," Dee Dee explained, "and then stopped up at the Twentieth-Century office to talk about a property, but all that talk made me hungry, so we came here."

"We're thinking of buying that play we saw tonight and turning it into a movie musical," Mr. TCF Number One said. "That is, if we can get Dee Dee to write the lyrics. Only she hasn't said yes yet."

"But she hasn't said no, either," Mr. TCF Number Two said. "It could be a great step for you, baby, careerwise, that is."

"Careerwise I'm doing just fine," Dee Dee said. "Hungerwise I'm about to faint. I'll have the steak, rare. What about you, Martine?"

"Steak Tartare for me," I said.

Mr. TCF Number One gave me a toothy grin, "A girl who likes raw meat. That's my kind of girl."

171

I almost changed my order to Eggs Benedict, well done, but Dee Dee put him in his place.

"Martine likes her Steak Tartare with caviar, don't you Martine? Do you have caviar?" she asked the waiter.

"Yes, ma'am. Beluga, Sevruga—"

"Beluga. That's the kind you usually have at home, isn't it, Martine?"

"Usually."

"Fine, bring my friend the Beluga with her Steak Tartare." She turned to Mr. TCF Number One, "After all, this is on the expense account, isn't it? And I've been working all evening. Midnight, and I haven't had my dinner. Have you eaten, Martine?"

"No," I said. "I've been working, too."

"What kind of work do you do?" Mr. TCF Number One asked.

"Martine's a terrific writer," Dee Dee said. "And let's talk about that. If you want me to do the lyrics for that show, maybe you should think about Martine doing the screen treatment."

Dee Dee had managed to change the tenor of the evening. From a sexy, flirty conversation the mood swung to one of business. I was grateful. After that nonevent with Peregrine I was thinking seriously of entering a convent.

CHAPTER XXII

Andy

While the weekend with Janet failed to renew our early relationship and marriage vows, it did clear up my doubts and confusions about how she felt toward me and how I felt about her. It was undeniable: we had an arrangement, not a marriage.

Nevertheless, my feelings of guilt about seeing Martine were diminishing. I was seeing her more frequently and with less secrecy. We'd meet for lunch often, sometimes in a restaurant, sometimes at her apartment where we'd make much love and eat little. It was all delicious. We would also meet for drinks after work even on the days we'd been together for lunch.

I was constantly on the lookout for little presents. Every time I'd pass a store window I would check to see if there was anything she would like. Not big things, but things like toys or funny stuffed dolls. I would often bring her flowers because we both loved them, almost any kind.

But she always compared them to the five-foot, grotesque paper rose she kept in a long-necked Tiffany vase that stood in solitary splendor in a prominent place in her living room. It was the first thing you noticed when you entered the room. It demanded your attention. No matter what I sent or brought, she'd compare it to the perfect rose. She said she would keep it forever. The thought was sweet, but hardly realistic. Even though it was made of wire and paper, it would deteriorate eventually, and besides, nothing lasts forever. If we ever broke up, God forbid, I was sure she would throw the rose away.

Everything in my life—my wife, my job, even my kids became secondary to Martine. I'd never experienced such prolonged ecstasy. Martine cared about me. Whenever I was at her apartment she wanted me to be happy. She had our favorite drinks and little things to eat, always delicious.

Martine tried to adjust her schedule to mine, and because she was a free-lance writer she could do so some of the time. And when she couldn't and I couldn't see her, I missed her so much it hurt.

My relationship with Janet grew more distant and formal. I went through the routine of the husband and father mechanically.

I took care of the kids on weekends, went to the dinner parties we were invited to, hosted the dinner parties we gave. I examined our friends and discovered that for the most part they were Janet's, and I didn't really like them.

Janet and I slept in the same bed, but we had no

sex. I had always initiated it, and since I was no longer interested, it stopped. Janet didn't seem to mind because she never commented. Of course she noticed it, and a lot of other things, too.

One evening I arrived home about eight. I had called and told Janet I was working late, but I had been with Martine. I let myself into the apartment and called out, "I'm home." Janet was in the bathroom where the girls were finishing their baths. She came out of the bathroom and walked rapidly towards me, her eyes filled with rage, and between clenched teeth she shouted,

"Where have you been? With that cunt Martine again?"

It was like a slap in the face, as it was meant to be. This was the moment I thought I had been waiting for. Here was my chance to make my break—sudden, in the heat of anger, not in reasoned discussion. But was I ready for the moment? Stalling, and still shocked by her verbal onslaught, I said, "What are you talking about?"

"Fire Island isn't on the moon, you know. We have phones and the Yellow Pages. And when enough people told me that they had seen you around town, and always with the same girl, I hired a private detective. Do you think I'm blind and stupid?"

After that, everything just poured out of me. The relief of no more secrets, the need to counterattack, my indignation at being spied upon, the realization that Janet had never loved me—all came together.

"Okay, I was with Martine—because I love her—I love being with her—"

"Is that so? Well, you have a family, two girls you're

175

responsible for, and you're married to me, and from now on you're going to stop seeing her and stop spending money on fancy dinners and flowers for her, or else—"

"Or else what?"

"Why the hell did you make me have children? So I'd be stuck at home with them? And you'd have the chance to fuck around with other women?"

We stood toe-to-toe in the hallway shouting at each other. When she mentioned the children I remembered they were in the bathroom, undoubtedly hearing every word.

"Stop yelling, the kids'll hear us," I said.

"I don't give a damn. Let them hear. Let them know what a son-of-a-bitch their father is. And if you don't stop seeing her, I'll really let them know what kind of a man their father is. They'll never want to see you or talk to you again."

"You're perfect, I suppose? What kind of a wife are you? You don't give a shit about me and never have. Dick Templeton threw you over and you got me on the third bounce. Just because you spread your legs for me, I owe you my life. That's a pretty high price for a fuck. Let me tell you something, Martine really cares for me, not as a meal ticket or an escort. With you, I'm nothing!"

"I've done my job, ask anybody. I had your children, I made a nice home for you, I entertain your boss. I want you to do your job. That's it."

That was it for me. This had been my life with Janet, living by her rules and her commands. Now here it was, our marriage stated in clear, unmistakable terms.

I felt a release in my head and my body, a physical

176

feeling. I understood as I never had before why Martine had to exist in my life.

"You don't care about me and you never have. I'm getting out of here."

"If you leave now, you'll regret it the rest of your life. I'm not going to let two men walk out on me. I'll make your life so miserable—"

I never heard the rest of the sentence. I slammed the door behind me. I didn't wait for the elevator. I just ran down the stairs into the street where I stood gulping air as if I had been running. I'd never had a fight like that before with anyone. I had never stood up to Janet like that, either. I was free of her—it had finally happened. I hadn't consciously planned it, but now I was free to be with Martine. I was free. I felt exhilarated. I had practical problems to deal with, but I didn't care. I would support Janet and the girls, but I didn't have to live with Janet. I didn't have to hide anymore or look over my shoulder when I was with Martine. My double life was over. I was free of a loveless marriage—I never knew how much I had hated that marriage until this moment. I felt very good.

I went to a nearby bar to settle down and to think about my next move and my future. I was now free to do as I pleased. No matter what alternative ideas I had, the most pleasing idea was to call Martine. She hadn't expected to hear from me. We had parted just a short time earlier, and she knew I had gone home.

"What's the matter?" she asked. "Is everything all right? Are you all right?"

"I did it. I've left Janet. We had a fight. She knows about you and me. A lot more than we might think. She must have had me followed. She knows your name and where you live, she probably knows your phone number.''

''It doesn't matter, I don't care. Are you all right? Come over, please.''

''Do you want me? Do you really want me?''

''Oh yes, I want you. Please come.''

''All right. I'll come now. I'm coming now.''

CHAPTER XXIII

Martine

What was I letting myself in for?

Nothing turned out the way I had thought it would.

Summer ended and I was sure that Andy and I had ended as well. We would go on seeing each other for a while, I thought, but that would taper off. At first we would see each other once or twice a week, and then once a week, and then once every two weeks, and finally we wouldn't see each other at all. Not ever again. It was time I learned to be more tough and realistic. I had known what the ending would be when I started this romance with a married man and father of two. Why should it be any different for us than for the hundreds of summer romances that end after Labor Day?

Dee Dee went to the coast to do a stint for a new group of Twentieth Century-Fox films, and I saw her off at the splashy TWA terminal at Kennedy.

"And don't forget, when What's-his-face stops calling, get on a plane and come out to the coast. You may change your mind about the place. Lots of money to be made there. Lots of men to be made there, too."

"Not for me."

"You may change your mind when the phone stops ringing."

"Maybe it won't."

"Oh sure," Dee Dee said, "and Central Park is filled with unicorns nibbling the tulips. Have you seen any unicorns lately, Martine? Grow up."

I felt so dumb. There were tears in my eyes.

"Oh, for God's sake," Dee Dee said, "if you're going to start that I won't be able to get on the fucking plane."

"I'm fine. I'm just sorry to see you go."

Dee Dee nodded. She knew that I meant it. We didn't agree about everything, but we were friends, easy with each other, and noncritical, and I wondered who I would talk to once she was on the coast. Andy would float away from me gradually; I was sure about that, no matter what I said to Dee Dee, and now Dee Dee was flying out to California. It was going to be a lonely fall, and I didn't have much hope for the winter.

"I'll call you when I find out where I'm staying," Dee Dee said. "There are worse places than sunny California. Promise me that you'll think about it."

"I'll think about it."

And then Dee Dee's flight was called, and I left the terminal and caught a cab back to the city.

"How about it, darling," the cab driver asked. "You mind if I take someone else back to New York in the same cab?"

Doubling up riders is against the law in New York,

180

as both of us knew. "Does that mean we'll split the fare on the meter?" I asked. I was heartbroken but not crazy.

The cab driver threw the clock, moved into gear, and slammed out of the terminal.

"I didn't know you was from New York," he said. "I thought maybe you was from out of town."

"Sorry."

"I'm just trying to make a living, lady."

He was silent after that, and I was grateful. My friend Phyllis spends most of the year in Mexico City, but when she visits New York she starts out every short taxi ride by giving the cab driver a one-dollar bill.

"What's that for?" she's asked.

"I've got a bad headache," she answers. Or sometimes she says, "I have a serious problem that I'm trying to solve, and I need quiet, so if you'll refrain from talking to me I'll match that dollar at the end of the ride."

I'm always sure that a cab driver is going to throw her out of his car for being insulting, but it hasn't happened yet.

"Two dollars isn't a lot of money," Phyl says, "if you consider how much dumb conversation I've avoided."

I was so grateful to the cab driver for driving me home in angry silence that I overtipped him. His thank you was almost inaudible; after all, I had stopped him from making twice as much money as he felt he was entitled to.

When I got home something happened that made me wish I could call Dee Dee. I would have told her

181

that unicorns do roam in Central Park and if she hadn't seen one it was because she wasn't looking.

Andy called. I knew something had happened the moment I heard his voice. He was shouting and his voice was shaking. This wasn't the first time he had called me when he was supposed to be with Janet. When they went to a movie he called me from the lobby where he had gone pretending to need a cigarette.

Once he had called me from the ballet during intermission.

"I miss you," was what he said each time. "I miss you."

"You better hurry back to the theater," I said the time he had called from Lincoln Center. "They won't let you back to your seat if the ballet has started."

"Who cares?"

But this time he sounded different. Excited, frightened, nervous. I had trouble making out his words. My God, my heart was pounding, what if he was sick? What if he had been in an accident? I would go to the hospital, I wouldn't care what Janet or anyone else said, I would go to him.

"Andy, what is it? What's wrong? Where are you?"

"I'm in a pay phone. On the street. Martine, I've left Janet—really left her. Martine, did you hear me?"

"Yes, Andy—look, what do you want to do? Do you want to come over here?"

"Yes, can I? Do you want me? Do you really want me?"

"Yes—I want you. I do want you—"

"I'm on my way," Andy said, "I'm coming home."

We hung up, and my heart was pounding more than

ever. I was in a panic. What was I letting myself in for? Where would he stay? With me, I supposed. But I hadn't lived with anyone for years; I didn't know if I was ready for it. The last person I had lived with— really lived with—was Davy. Luckily, it had been in a different apartment, and in a different bed. True, Andy had stayed with me during part of the summer, but I had thought it was temporary. Now he would be moving in. What about his wife and kids? Would I have to cope with them? And I thought of the people I knew. My friends, my mother.

My mother hadn't been feeling well lately, and I had insisted that she spend more time with me. My father had died five years earlier, and I panicked at the idea that my mother might be ill enough to die. I remembered how often she would say to me that she didn't want me to be alone. Did she have a premonition, or had she been seeing doctors without telling me?

I knew how devoted Andy was to his kids, it was a devotion that he expected me to understand completely. Yet, whenever I spoke of my mother, my parents, he looked blank. His parents were hard, cold people. He couldn't believe that my parents were not.

I hoped that my mother and Andy would like each other. They didn't know it, but they shared many tastes, many opinions. Nevertheless, they would be meeting at the wrong time. Andy had his problems, my mother had hers, neither would see each other as I saw each of them.

I went into my bedroom and began moving clothes from my big walk-in closet to a smaller closet. No, that didn't make sense. I started doing things the other way around. I would move my clothes from the small closet

183

into the big closet, and then Andy could have a closet all to himself. And what about bureau drawers? My hair hung down, and I was sweating. It was crazy. Why was I so scared? Just a few hours ago I had been mooning about like a heartbroken teenager who'd lost her steady, and now that Andy was on his way—maybe on his way to be mine forever—I was frightened. Me, the most involved, committed person in the world— hell, I became involved with a red balloon and committed to a paper rose. Was I afraid to become committed to another person?

When the doorbell rang I ran and opened the door. I think he had run all the way to get to me, and then I was in his arms and I wasn't scared any more.

I nestled against his chest. "I'm glad you're here."

Andy looked around as though he had never seen the place before.

"I've come home," he said.

My heart was beating fast again. "Where are your things? I've been making room in my closet."

Andy sat down. "No things. I just left. Martine, do you really want me?"

"Of course."

"I mean *me*. Do you want *me*?"

"Andy," I sat down beside him and tried to hug all of him to me, "I want you."

My heart and his heart slowed down together. At least we both stopped gasping for breath at about the same time.

"It's all right, then," Andy said, and he leaned back, his eyes shut.

His face frightened me. He looked exhausted,

184

drained. I sat beside him just holding his hand until he opened his eyes again.

"It's like getting out of jail," he said. "Even freedom is a shock."

"What about the kids?"

He shook his head. "I'll have to tell them. Maybe when I go back for my things."

He looked so sad that I didn't know what to do for him.

"It's going to be all right," I said. "You'll see, it'll work out."

"Can we go to bed?" Andy said. "I'm so tired all of a sudden. Can we lie down?"

I led him into the bedroom, and after he stretched out he was in a deep sleep in about ten minutes. I lay down beside him, wide awake. He was lying face down, and he lay so still that for a scary minute I was afraid that he had stopped breathing.

"Andy?" I leaned over him. "Andy?"

He turned, still asleep, and gathered me to him. With his arms around me, he pillowed my head against his chest.

"I know what you want," he murmured, still asleep, "you want this. You want a cocoon. Don't worry, I'll be your cocoon."

My head was on his chest, and I could feel each breath he took. Andy wanted to create a cocoon for me; it was lovely, and it was what I wanted. But was it possible? His wife, his children, my mother, earning a living—we both needed a cocoon, but I doubted that the world would let us retreat into one.

185

CHAPTER XXIV

Andy

Martine was slightly disheveled when I arrived. It took me only ten minutes after I had called her, and she had obviously been trying to straighten the apartment. She had been working when I called. She studied my face when I arrived, and then threw herself at me and wrapped her arms about me.

"Sit down and let me make you a drink. You must need one. Then give me a minute and let me get myself together."

She took only a couple of minutes but she had combed her hair and put on a robe she knew I liked.

"What happened?"

I told her as best as I could. I couldn't repeat all the details of the fight, they were too painful, but the meaning and the result were clear to Martine. The phone started to ring. Martine made no move to answer it. It rang every ten minutes and for a very long time each time. Martine and I both knew who it was.

"What are you going to do?" she asked.

"I guess see a lawyer. I'll support Janet and the kids, and I'll need a place to see them. Martine, can I stay here? With you?"

"Of course."

That solved one problem. But what about my kids? I remembered that a friend of mine, Tim Bell, had an apartment in Greenwich Village he didn't use very often. It was in an old tenement and had two rooms, a kitchen and a combination living room-bedroom. I'd had drinks with him there a number of times. Tim had asked me to share the rent with him and said I could use the apartment whenever or however I wanted to.

Time lived in the affluent suburb of Westport with his wife and two sons. He took the apartment in town because he liked to play around and he found hotel rooms were expensive or sometimes unavailable. He also had violent fights with his wife and would storm out of the house and not return for several days. The apartment served both his purposes well.

I told Martine about Tim's apartment. "I could take the girls there on weekends—that is, if Janet lets me have them on weekends."

I called Tim the following morning and he was delighted at my offer to share the apartment and its costs. He told me he hardly used the apartment, and never on weekends. I offered to have it cleaned and kept clean and I went to look at it that night. It was a mess. The sofa bed in the living room looked as if it had been rejected by the Salvation Army. The floors were covered with worn linoleum, and there were chromium-legged kitchen chairs and a Formica-topped table. There was also a bookcase with about fifty books, all on self-improvement. *How To Fly a Plane, How to Be a Stockbroker, How To Play Tennis, How To Live To Be One Hundred, How To Be a Successful Photographer, How To Win at Poker*.

The refrigerator contained two half-filled jars of olives. There was one closet and one chest. One drawer of the chest was occupied by Tim's clothes. The closet had some ancient camera equipment; Tim had been interested in photography at one time. It certainly wasn't the apartment "The Odd Couple" inhabited on television. And it wasn't the apartment I had just left behind. But it was a place where I could be with my kids.

Janet was as good as her word. She mounted a campaign and attacked me on all fronts. We fought the battle of money, the children, my family, her family, the company I worked for, and our friends, who quickly became her allies. Her objective was to make me live up to my responsibilities as she saw them.

I wasn't completely helpless. For one thing, I was expecting her onslaught. Having lived with her for eight years, I was aware of her force of will. Now that I was out from under, I felt a sense of my own strength and determination. I also had Martine behind me, and I knew her love would sustain me. It didn't take too long to discover Martine was the only ally I had.

I called Janet to tell her I was going to come by to pick up my clothes. I suggested I do this when she wasn't home in order to avoid a confrontation again in front of the kids. She said she would let me come on

189

the following Sunday when she would be visiting her mother. However, she added one condition.

"I want you to come to a marriage counselor with me."

I was sure that no marriage counselor would tell us to get back together, so I told Janet to make the appointment. It might make life easier if she heard from a neutral party that we didn't belong together.

"I've already made an appointment. It's for next Wednesday, ten in the morning. You can pick up your clothes this Sunday afternoon. I'll leave your luggage on the bed, but don't take anything else from the apartment—nothing but your clothes."

I didn't tell her that I didn't want anything from that apartment. I was apprehensive when I went for my clothes, but the apartment was empty. Janet and the children were not at home. She did say she wouldn't be there, but I couldn't trust what she said.

On the bed was an old duffel bag and a torn suitcase. This, Janet had decided, was my luggage. Fuck her, let her keep the rest of the luggage.

I emptied my bureau and the closet of my clothes, and stuffed my belongings into the duffel bag and suitcase. I noticed my favorite black sweater was missing. It wasn't in my dresser, so I went through Janet's dresser. There it was, nestled in a drawer beneath other sweaters. I added my sweater to the duffel bag. I looked around the apartment one last time to see if there was anything I had forgotten. I saw my books and records. I remembered Janet's admonition and decided I'd pick them up another time. No need to antagonize Janet further. She'd notice if even one book was missing. I left with only my clothes stuffed hurriedly into the bag and torn suitcase.

The first person I told of my split with Janet was my brother Peter. Peter was two years younger than I. We didn't see much of each other, but I felt closer to him than any other member of my family. He had a moderately successful dental practice, and lived in Queens with his wife, and a surly son who he told me was a pain in the ass.

He took the news of my split calmly. We talked about a lawyer and he suggested I see John Light, a mutual friend of ours. John isn't a divorce lawyer, but both Peter and I had faith in him as a friend and as an attorney. John had originally been my friend; I had introduced him to Peter and they became close friends and saw each other often.

"John will be sympathetic and he'll help. He just got a divorce himself. By the way, are you planning a divorce, or is this just a fight and a trial separation?"

"Probably a divorce. I know Janet will fight it tooth and nail. Right now I want to get my head clear, and I need a little time."

"Is there another woman?"

I hesitated, and said, "No."

I didn't want to talk about Martine just yet.

"Okay. But don't do anything rash until we get together. I want to talk to you, Andy."

I was beginning to feel badly that I hadn't told Peter the truth. Hadn't told him that there *was* another woman—one I was really in love with. I wasn't feeling too good about denying Martine.

I went to John Light's office on Saturday. He greeted me very warmly, put his arm around my shoulder, and led me into his office. I sat in a chair facing his desk, feeling tense, and also a little relieved because now I'd have another ally to help me sort things out. And John was an ally who knew what he was doing. I was paying him, but I felt comforted because he was my friend as well as my lawyer.

Things started badly when he said, "I'm sorry to hear about you and Janet. How are the kids taking it?"

Why was he sorry? Maybe what had happened was a good thing for me. I appreciated his concern about my kids, though.

"I can't really tell," I said, "I've seen them a few times since I left. They seem all right and they're always glad to see me."

"Tell me what happened and what you want me to do," he said.

I took a deep breath. "The situation is quite simple. I've been living a loveless marriage. I've gone over it in my mind for months—even before I left Janet. We don't care for each other, it's as simple as that. Look, you and I have known each other for years, we don't spend much time together, but you've been to my house for dinner—though not lately."

"Yes, I remember. It seemed you and Janet got along all right. And your kids are great little girls."

"Well, we didn't get along all right. What you couldn't know was that before dinner Janet and I would have a big fight, and after the guests left we'd have a bigger fight. Janet always found something to criticize me about. Something I had done that embarrassed her in front of our guests. Let me tell you something, for over two years I haven't invited anyone to my home."

"But you give dinner parties, don't you?"

"Yes. But they're initiated by Janet, and she makes up the guest list. Whatever friends I may have had I don't have anymore. I've led two lives, one at home and one outside. But only recently have I realized and understood the division. I've found another woman who's the complete opposite of Janet. She's warm, she's kind, she's generous. She loves me and shows it to me all the time."

"So she's the real reason you left Janet?"

"Let's say she's the trigger. What you don't know is that I've had other women during my marriage, but I didn't leave Janet. Because every time I was with another woman I'd compare her to Janet, and fantasize about her as a wife. Not just in bed, because in bed they were almost all better than Janet. They all failed in my eyes until Martine. Don't you see? I was looking. I was unhappy and dissatisfied, there was something missing from my life."

"How do you feel about your new friend, what's-her-name?"

"Martine. I love her."

"Are you sure it's not just sex and passion? The seven-year itch that all men seem to go through? How long have you been seeing her?"

"It's been five months now."

"Listen, Andy, I want to talk to you not as your lawyer but as your friend. Maybe a tough divorce lawyer wouldn't say this to you, but I've got to. Do you think an affair of five months should break up an eight-year marriage? Especially when you've got two kids."

"John, you haven't been listening to me. I'm trying to tell you my marriage is no good. It's over. It wasn't

193

good before I met Martine. But I settled. I didn't know there was anyone like Martine out there.''

"Do you want to marry her?"

"I think so."

"But you're not sure."

"I'm pretty sure."

"Andy, I'm your friend, and I know what you're going through. You know Sandy and I just got divorced, but maybe you don't know why I married her. It was because of guilt. We had been living together for three years and I felt I owed her. It was a lousy reason to get married. Don't you make the same mistake. Think about it. Meanwhile, what do you want me to do about Janet and the girls?"

"I'll support them. How do I do it?"

"Well, you can't expect Janet to go back to work right away. It's not that easy to find a job if you haven't worked for six years. You'll have to support her in the style she's living in now."

"John, I've only got a salary. I make a good living, but it's finite. I've got to live, too. You know, now I'll have two rents to pay, and other expenses."

"You don't want to take anything away from the kids, do you?"

"Of course not."

"I'll tell you what. You give Janet and the kids as much as you can. Try keeping it at the same level as before. That doesn't mean you'll always have to give her that much money. The amount you give her now won't prejudice any final arrangements. That means if you go to court it won't have any bearing on the final settlement."

"I can live with that, but I know Janet, she's vin-

194

dictive. She's going to create additional expenses. She'll come after me till I'm strangled.''

"Come on now, she's not that bad. Remember, I know Janet. You're both going through a crisis in your marriage, and like most crises, it'll blow over. Try to think calmly and rationally. Try not to see Martine too much, and don't do anything hasty. Go see a marriage counselor and I'll help you work things out with Janet.''

When I left John's office I didn't feel too reassured. He thought he knew Janet, but I knew he didn't. Then again, he said he would handle matters, and that would make my life easier. I didn't take his advice about Martine, though. John didn't know that while I had an apartment in which I could see my kids, I was living with Martine.

When I got to Martine's she asked what had happened at John's office. I told her about the temporary financial arrangements that John had recommended and that I agreed to. Then I told her laughingly that John had said my feelings toward her were based on guilt.

"Are they?''

"Damn it, they're not! How can you ask me such a stupid question?''

"You seemed to accept that idea from him.''

"I did not! I just didn't want to discuss our relationship with him.'' Martine went into the kitchen, poured herself some wine and came back into the living room.

"What do you intend to do now?'' she asked.

"Nothing,'' I yelled. "I've made enough decisions for one day. Don't push me. Eight years down the drain. Now I'm ending it. Isn't that enough for one day?''

Martine didn't yell back. "Andy, it's not too late: you can still go back to Janet. Dee Dee is dying to have me come out to California and stay with her for awhile. Maybe if I went away it'd be easier for you."

"No, please don't go—then I'd have nobody. I'm sorry I yelled, Martine. It's just that I feel so pressured I had to let out steam, and I've nobody left but you, so I yelled at you."

Trying to make amends I went to her chair, knelt down, and put my head in her lap. "Look, we have the rest of the day, a whole day to spend together with no obligations to anybody. Let's not spoil it, let's go down to the Village. Take a walk, look at the shops and the people. Then we'll have dinner there, okay?"

She looked down at me, smiled hesitantly, stroked my head a few times, and agreed. We went down to the Village, and I showed Martine the apartment I was sharing with Tim Bell. The shabby furnishings didn't bother her as they did me.

Now that I'd left my family I had to let a number of people know my new address. I decided to have my mail forwarded to Tim's apartment. I didn't want any business or personal mail going to my old apartment where Janet was certain to open all letters. I asked Brenda to come into my office the following morning and told her to shut the door behind her. She sat across from my desk, pencil poised.

"Brenda, I need your help. I've split with my wife and I'm now living in an apartment on Washington Place. I want you to send a change of address to a list of people I'll give you. You'd better notify personnel, too."

I gave Brenda some further instructions which she

quickly made note of. I was pleased that she hadn't said she was sorry about my marital breakup. Everybody else did. I'm sure they thought it was the right thing to say, but it wasn't. I had left Janet, and I felt it was a good thing, and nothing to be sorry about.

"Is there anything else, boss?" Brenda asked.

"Yes, I'm afraid you're about to become involved in my problems. Janet will call here a lot of times, and you're going to have to take her calls. I'll tell you if I want to talk to her or not. I don't want you to get into any conversations with her. If I'm not in, take a message. But there will be times you'll have to tell her I'm not in when I'll be here; will you do that?"

"Sure, no problem. I can handle that. What else?"

"One more thing, can you order lunch for me today? I don't feel like going out—get me a hamburger with a slice of raw onion, french fries, and a Tab."

"Raw onions? How can you eat that stuff?" She gave an exaggerated shudder of disgust, then added, "Do you want company? I plan to eat in, too."

"Sure, be my guest."

It might be pleasant to listen to Brenda chatter about her friends and social life, which seemed abundant. She was also privy to all the office gossip, some of it not so dull.

When lunch arrived she brought it into the office and laid it out on the desk. I noticed she had ordered the identical lunch to mine, including the raw onion. She bit lustily into her hamburger.

"How's the onion?" I asked.

"Not so bad. It takes a little getting used to."

I felt I'd found a new friend.

"By the way," she asked, "how did you find an

apartment in the Village? I've been looking for an apartment of my own for months. I'm tired of sharing one. Fran is my best friend, but we're getting on each other's nerves. I'm too old for sorority life.''

"I didn't find it. It belongs to a friend of mine who uses it only occasionally and he's letting me live there.''

"Are there any vacant apartments in the building?''

"I doubt it, but I'll ask the super, if I can find him.''

"What's the block like?''

"There are some pretty buildings and some old ones, like the one I live in. But it's near the park and it's only fifteen minutes to the office. I think it's kind of nice.''

"I think I'll look for an apartment down there. I'll go Saturday and canvass all the buildings. Maybe I'll get lucky.''

CHAPTER XXV

Andy

Janet called to remind me about the appointment with the marriage counselor. I told her I'd be there as promised, but I was reluctant to go. What if you don't want to keep your marriage together? What if staying married is a bad idea? If this marriage counselor was worth anything, she'd see that Janet and I didn't belong together.

The marriage counselor was a tired-looking woman in her mid-forties. If she talked to people like me and Janet all day long, it was no wonder she seemed spent. Janet was already in her office when I arrived, and the counselor's greeting to me was quite cold. She didn't smile. I sat down in a chair next to Janet, and we faced the counselor.

"What can I do for you?" she asked.

Janet started right in.

"As you know, I was the one who called for the appointment, my husband didn't want to come."

"So?"

Only slightly ruffled by the counselor's lack of sympathetic reaction, Janet ploughed on.

"We've been married eight years, and we have two daughters . . ." Janet told the story of our marriage in detail. The counselor asked a few questions and made a few notes. I stayed silent. It didn't matter to me whether Janet was accurate or not, or how one-sided her presentation was. I was sullen, disinterested, and I wanted to be out of there.

"I know I worry about money a lot," Janet was saying, "Andy is in such an insecure business. I may have given him a bad time once or twice when he was out of a job or when he wanted to change jobs. And he has such erratic hours, he's often late for dinner. He also has to travel out of town."

"Do you have to travel a lot?" The counselor turned to me.

"I have one client in Ohio and I do have to visit him. Then he comes to New York, and I take him out to dinner; it happens to be part of the job."

She turned back to Janet. "Is that the only problem?"

Janet paused as though she didn't want to tell about it. Finally she blurted out, "My husband's left me for another woman."

"Why do you think he did that?"

That question got my attention; I hadn't expected it. I sat up and began to take an interest.

"He's never satisfied. He likes to read a lot, and he

200

thinks writers are gods. His girlfriend is a writer, and he thinks she's a lot more than she really is."

The counselor turned to me. "Why did you leave your wife?"

My answer was ready; I'd been considering it. "It wasn't a sudden decision. I've been thinking about it for a long time. Janet and I don't love each other, and I found someone whom I love and who loves me. It's that simple."

"Well?" she asked Janet.

"I've tried to be a good wife. We have two wonderful children. God knows what will happen to them if Andy leaves. I work hard, I keep house, take care of the children, cook, and entertain. I sleep with Andy when he wants to. Isn't that enough?"

"Janet, what do you think are the basic differences between you and Andy?"

Janet answered, "I know how hard the real world is. I come from a broken home, and I know what it's like to have a part-time father. When I was a kid we never were sure of money, my father couldn't be depended upon. My mother had to go to work because my father wasted his money on get-rich-quick schemes and other women. My sister and I had to work after school while we were in high school; we were the only girls on the block who had to do this, and it was humiliating.

"I don't want this to happen to my daughters. If Andy would only settle down—or just settle for what he's got. He's always reaching for something bigger, reaching for the stars, he calls it. I look at the ground in front of me. I'm willing to settle."

"Settle for what? Why should you settle?" the counselor asked. Then she turned to me. "Is that how you see the differences between you?"

"Basically, yes. Janet's always upset if I change jobs. I lost my job once, and she went crazy. But I've always supported her and the kids, and I expect to go on doing so. I'm no visionary, but I do reach for better things. Janet's right, I'm almost never satisfied, I'm curious and I want more. That's part of the fun of life, exploring. If I fail I can bounce back, I always have."

"He gets so enthusiastic about new projects," Janet said. "And when they don't work out he's disappointed and goes into a depression which lasts for days. Don't get excited is what I say, and then you won't be disappointed, but Andy never listens to me."

This wrangling went on a little longer, and the counselor asked Janet "But why should you or he settle for what you've got if you're not satisfied with it? Do you settle because you think it's all you're entitled to? You seem to want a civil service worker for a husband. But I don't think he's that kind of man.

"I think you should start therapy, Janet. If you like, I can recommend a psychologist. See him for a few months and then come back here for another discussion if you want to."

The counselor turned to me, "I would suggest you continue to see your children as often as you can. And try not to have any fights in front of them."

That was the end of marriage counseling. The counselor didn't advise that we try to stay together. I was stunned.

If the marriage counselor surprised me, so did my buddy, Jim O'Donnell. He asked me to lunch one day, and I told him the news about me, Janet, and Martine.

His manner, usually jovial and conspiratorial, suddenly became avuncular and pompous.

"Andy, Andy, Andy. Why did you do that? Janet was all right. She's not a bad-looking woman. And what about the kids?"

"I'm tired of hearing 'What about the kids.' Everytime I tell somebody about my split I hear 'What about the kids.' The kids'll be fine. They'll be better off without me and Janet living together and killing each other. Our marriage was no model marriage."

"That's the trouble. You read too many fairy tales when you were a kid. 'And they all lived happily ever after.' That's a lot of crap. Your marriage is like my marriage, but you don't see me getting separated and divorced. I play around, but so does every other guy I know. Martine's okay, but you don't have to leave your family for her."

To this day, I don't know why I didn't let him have it. Instead, I got defensive.

"Jim, Martine isn't just another lay to me. If our marriages are typical, maybe marriage isn't for me. I'm not saying I'm going to marry Martine right away. What I am saying is that she's terrific."

Jim wouldn't let it go. Over his second drink he said, "Andy, you've made a mistake. It's okay to play around, but you should never get involved."

A lot of thoughts ran through my head while he was talking, mostly about Martine and me. I thought of what I felt for her, how good the sex was, how I loved her. But somehow I couldn't say the word *love*. It would have seemed out of place with Jim. He would have dismissed that as another fairy tale. I suddenly felt the word was very private. *Love.* A secret to be shared only by Martine and me.

"Have you moved in with Martine?" Jim asked.

"I'm sharing Tim Bell's apartment officially, but I'm living with Martine."

Jim's face lit up. "Tim Bell is letting you share his apartment? That's great. Why don't you and I party there? I'll get us a couple of girls—"

"You mean Ilona has a friend?"

"No, not Ilona. If she finds out you left your wife, she's liable to get some ideas about me. I'll get other girls. Don't worry, I can find them. How big is the apartment?"

"Just one bed."

"That's okay. It'll be a warm, intimate party. What do you say?"

"I'm pretty busy—we'll talk about it some other time."

CHAPTER XXVI

Martine

I couldn't believe what Andy brought to my apartment from the apartment he had been living in with Janet for—how long?—better than eight years. There was one battered suitcase with a worn strap holding it together, and one small airline bag. There was also his guitar and some books of guitar music.

"I guess you'll get your records and books later," I said.

"I don't want anything," Andy said, "nothing."

He didn't want or take anything. But he did get bills. Bills to reupholster the couch (in cream wide-wale corduroy, Andy told me), bills for new drapery from Lord & Taylor, dentist bills, doctor bills, and of course, Janet's lawyer's bills.

There's a fine line between being a man's mistress and being a man's wife. Wives, the stories tell us, nag, complain, demand. Mistresses are warm, seductive, and undemanding. Of course, there were mistresses in the good old days (or bad old days, however you want to think of it) who demanded furs and jewels and considerable real estate just to be mistresses.

But that kind of thinking is old-fashioned. Today's modern mistress is self-supporting and very often helps support the man who has made her his significant other.

I tried not to say anything, but I couldn't remain completely silent when Andy showed me the daily quota of bills that came to his office.

"I can understand the doctor, and the dentist, and the lawyer, and Barbara's psychiatrist. But re-covering the couch? And new drapes? Why should you pay for them?"

"They're for the new apartment." Andy's voice was so soft that I didn't think I had heard him.

"Did you say new apartment?"

"Yes."

"What new apartment?"

"Well, before I ever met you, Martine, I had put a deposit down on a co-op apartment. Three bedrooms and two baths. I want my kids to have their own rooms. I remember when I was a kid, I had to share a room with my two brothers. It was terrible. I never had any privacy. I want them to have that, Martine, the apartment. I'm making the down payment. It's the least I can do. You do understand, don't you?"

"Sure I understand."

And I did. Andy felt so guilty. No use telling him that he hadn't killed anyone. No use saying that the kids would be better off in the long run, that seeing their parents fight all the time was not exactly conducive to their happiness. No use telling him anything. Though I could have told him about guilt, if he had been willing to listen. My guilt about Davy, whom I had abandoned to death while I continued my life. My guilt about my father. The things I shouldn't have said, the things left undone.

And right now, my current guilt about my mother. Because my mother was very sick. She had gone to two doctors without me, but it was clear that her illness was no small matter, and I finally learned the details from my cousin Katy.

"She didn't want you to know she was sick," Katy said, "so I went to the doctors with her."

"What did they say?"

Katy didn't answer me.

"It can't be." My father had died of cancer a few years before. It wasn't possible for my mother to have the same disease. "Katy?"

"Yes," Katy said, "they think it is that."

That. I knew what that was, knew it without hearing the actual word. I felt as though I were suffocating.

"Does she know?" I asked.

"No, at least I don't think so. All she keeps saying is, 'Don't tell Martine, don't tell Martine.' But I had to tell you. I did, didn't I, Martine? You had to know."

"Yes, of course." My throat felt so dry I could hardly speak. I was a small child again, a child afraid of the dark. Don't leave me, Mommy.

But those were the words I never said to my mother. I never said that I knew how ill she was, and she never admitted to being that ill. I know that current theory embraces the idea of being completely honest with the dying, but I don't know whom that honesty serves. My

207

mother behaved as she always did and as she had brought me up to behave: with good manners. And manners meant not making the people you love unhappy or uncomfortable. We didn't weep on each other's shoulders, we didn't keen, we didn't wail. Except inside. It was a facade, true, but it was a facade created by love, by our care for each other.

I had trouble getting through each new day. There was Andy, whom I loved, crying on my shoulder. And there was my mother, whom I loved, not crying at all.

Andy's litany: constant, painful, increasingly guilt-filled, it was all about his children. I listened as long as I could, and then one day I said:

"They're alive, Andy, they're healthy kids. They're going to be fine. You haven't killed them, for heaven's sake."

"You don't understand. You don't have children—you're not a parent. You can't know. Martine, do you like children? I never even asked you that."

"Sure, I like nice children, kind children. Just as I like nice, kind people. Is there a different standard for kids?"

"You don't understand."

And I didn't.

If I didn't understand about Andy's kids, he didn't understand my feelings towards my mother. I didn't understand his guilt, he couldn't comprehend my panic. He had never been close to his parents, and he couldn't understand how I could be so close to mine. In America it's considered healthy to have a passion for one's children and unhealthy to love one's parents.

208

CHAPTER XXVII

Andy

After I left Janet I called to talk to the children every day, but first I would have to talk to Janet. Her conversation included sarcasm: "Is your fling over yet?" Or on the more practical side: "The washing machine broke down. What shall we do?" Suddenly Janet was helpless. Again. "The dishwasher broke down, and the repairman says we may not be able to repair it, we'll have to get a new one. I'll need some money." The collective *we* didn't elude me, but I ignored it, and money was a frequent subject. Even though the weekly check I sent Janet was more money than she had had when I was living with her, she was asking for still more. And there was the painful subject of the children.

"They keep asking for you. They want to know when you're coming home to stay."

The day that I told the kids that the separation between me and Janet was permanent was a day I'd rather forget. I said what every parent has said in the same circumstances. I told my daughters how much I loved them, that I would always love them. I was their father, I said, I would always be their father. No wonder men like Jim said they would never split from their wives. I kept repeating that the breakup had nothing to do with them, and that we would still see each other often.

"But where are you going?" Barbara asked. "How will I find you?"

"I'm not far from you, baby. I'm in another apartment, but it's right here in the city. I'll see you a lot of times, and we'll talk on the phone every day."

Diane was silent, I don't think she understood what I was saying, but Barbara wouldn't accept it.

"But you'll still come here every day, won't you?"

"Not every day, sweetheart, but I'll visit you often, and you'll visit me. You'll see. It'll be okay, I promise."

I kept on talking, and tears began forming in my eyes. My resolve was weakening as I began to see the meaning of my words getting through to them. Their faces began to look serious and solemn, particularly Barbara's.

"Your mother and I have not been getting along. We fight a lot. So I'm moving away. But it's not because I don't love you both. I love you more than anything in the world."

My tears began to choke me, and I was having trouble getting the words out coherently.

". . . want you to visit me . . . call you every day

. . . love you so much . . . I'm your daddy . . . always . . ."

Seeing me cry started the girls whimpering. Janet
finally got up from her chair, came up behind them
and put an arm around each of the girls.

"It has nothing to do with you. It's not your fault.
I love you." And she began to cry too.

Watching both their parents crying turned the girls'
whimpers into full wails. There were the four of us in
a small circle, me holding on to parts of the girls, and
Janet holding on to other parts, careful not to let our
hands touch. We were all sobbing and wailing when
Barbara slowed down enough to ask between sobs,
"Are you staying for dinner?"

My escape route. "No, baby, not tonight. I have to
go." I wiped tears from my face with my sleeve and
started composing myself. But when I got up the girls
wouldn't let go of my hands. I made my way slowly to
the door, a child on each side clutching me. I don't
know if I walked slowly because I was reluctant to go
or because they were holding me back, but the short
walk to the door took forever. Janet followed us, dab-
bing a tissue to her eyes. Finally at the door I crouched
down, my face level with theirs, took them both in my
arms and crushed them to me.

"Daddy loves you more than anything or anyone.
He's not moving away because he doesn't love you,
okay? I'll call you tomorrow and every day. Will you
talk to me? And I'll see you and you'll come see me."

I was holding them so tightly I began to affect their
breathing. They tried to pull away, so I let them go. I
turned to the door, opened it, and took one last look
back. Janet stood there with the girls standing close,

holding on to her legs; all crying. I shut the door behind me. I didn't wait for the elevator. I ran down the stairs, grateful they were badly lit. I wouldn't run into any of the neighbors I might have met in the elevator. The rest of the evening is a total blank.

CHAPTER XXVIII

Andy

Janet's lawyer was Jerry Goodman, who had been a friend of ours, or rather a friend of Janet's. Janet had met Cynthia Goodman in the playground, and our kids and their kids became playmates.

That daytime friendship soon blossomed into a day-and-evening relationship, so that we and the Goodmans had dinner together frequently. I was never too fond of them, but I went along with the dinners when Janet presented me with a *fait accompli.*

"We're having dinner with the Goodmans on Thursday at their house," or "The Goodmans are coming over tonight."

Jerry Goodman thought that Janet was terrific. His wife was the kind of person who could never make her mind up about anything. That's where Janet came in. She shopped with Cynthia, planned her party menus, told her what to wear when Jerry's boss was coming to dinner, and told her what to serve to important clients. Cynthia needed Janet's strength, and Jerry was grateful for her help.

"Andy, you are so lucky to have a wife like Janet," he told me more than once. "She's so decisive. I wish Cynthia were like that."

If Jerry thought Janet was pretty near perfect, he also thought I didn't deserve her. Most lawyers are overbearing and contentious, and Jerry was doubly so with me.

In any serious discussion he crossexamined me as though I were on the witness stand. This included discussions on politics, war, history, business, even the maintenance of Riverside Park or the state of the New York Yankees. As a result, I would try to keep the conversation inconsequential.

Jerry's need to dominate took the silliest forms. When he decided to buy a new car he offered to sell me his old one; he couldn't get the price he wanted from the car dealer. I didn't own a car because keeping a car in the city is as expensive a habit as cocaine. Everybody I knew owned a car and that's another reason I didn't own one. It was one way of proving that I wasn't like everyone else. I told Jerry I didn't want a car and thanked him for his offer. He persisted and kept telling me why I should buy it, why I needed it. When I continued to refuse, he demanded I give him satisfactory reasons as to why I was refusing his offer. Not having to see the Goodmans again was one of the side benefits of my separation from Janet.

"Andy, I just heard from Jerry Goodman," John Light called to tell me.

"What does he want?"

"It was a strange conversation. Not very professional."

"What did he say?" I asked.

"Did you ever have a fight with him?"

"No, but he thinks Janet is the perfect wife, and I'm sure he can't understand how I could leave her."

"That's it, then. He said some pretty nasty things about you."

"Like what?"

"It's not important. Let's get down to what Janet wants."

"It is important. I want to know what Jerry said."

"The usual four-letter words, and things like he'll see you starve, and what a rotten thing you did to your kids. He came on strong. I guess that's what happens when a client is also a friend, it's hard to act with professional detachment.

"Anyway, this is what they want: the same weekly money you gave Janet before you left, plus the rent, nursery school, all medical bills. That includes the analyst Janet is planning to see. I think that's fair so far, don't you?"

"Fair! That weekly household money included my expenses, too, like food, laundry, cleaning—"

"Okay, we'll get back to that. Janet also wants you to pay her department store bills and not close the accounts. She promises not to take advantage."

"Wouldn't she? John, what do you tell other husbands—clients who aren't your friends?"

"Normally, I tell them to close out their charge accounts."

"Why don't you tell me to do that? You're my lawyer. Aren't you supposed to protect me?"

"Don't be angry, Andy. I'm your friend. I'm acting as a conduit between you and Janet. I'm just telling you what she wants. I'm a lawyer, but I'm not a divorce lawyer."

"I'm closing out those accounts as soon as this conversation is over."

"Well," he paused a bit, "well, she said she bought a few things at Lord & Taylor. She says for the kids."

"How much?"

"Somewhere between three and four hundred dollars."

Jerry was going to keep his word. I was going to starve.

"What else does Janet want?"

"She wants the savings account, the checking account, half of what you have in mutual funds. She wants the co-op in her name, but you're to pay off the mortgage."

"She gets the house and I get the mortgage?"

"Andy, that's usual. Besides, I'm just telling you what she wants. It's negotiable. But first, let me tell you the whole thing."

"There's more?"

"She wants you to pay her phone bills. She said she was so upset when you walked out that she made a few long distance calls to her friend Nola in California."

"No! Enough!"

"Look—I have to tell you. She also says she needs new drapes for the living room."

"Did anybody say anything about a divorce?"

"It was brought up, but Janet and Jerry won't discuss it. They want you to agree to these requests, and

216

they want a formal separation agreement. Then they'll work out visiting rights for you to see the kids."

"What kind of visiting rights?"

"Janet wants you to take the girls to dinner every Wednesday, and she wants you to take them every weekend and holidays, except when she wants them. She'll let you know in advance, of course. She wants legal custody."

"Some custody. Would she like me to babysit for her two afternoons a week, too?"

"Andy, don't get sarcastic with me, it's not necessary."

"John, don't you see what Janet and Jerry are trying to do to me? First they want all my money, then they want to tie up my time, too. They're trying to bury me."

"I am a little surprised, it is a little too much. And one more thing—she wants you to pay the bill for her private investigator."

"Are you crazy? She has me followed and I'm supposed to pay for it?"

"Calm down. They could put it in as part of her legal fees—you know you have to pay her legal fees, don't you?"

"Did you leave anything out? Is there anything else?"

"Not right now."

"Wow! And I was afraid she was going to be unreasonable."

"There's no reason to get nasty. After all, Janet's all alone and she has two girls to bring up. She hasn't worked for years. And you do have Martine."

"John, I can't live with those demands—you know

217

that. If I give in to everything Janet's asking for, I'll be left with under a hundred dollars a week to live on.''

''But you're young, Andy. You have a good chance of earning more money, haven't you? By the way, they also wanted an escalator clause. If you earn more money, Janet's alimony goes up.''

''What if I earn less money, or if I lose my job—does the alimony go down?''

''No, but I put my foot down on the escalator clause, I said no to that.''

At last. ''What should I do?''

''Most of Janet's requests were pretty standard. The others—well, she's in a state of shock, so I say go along without signing anything. You don't have to pay the phone bill or buy the drapes. Nothing's on paper, and she'll calm down. And I'll see to it that any agreement you make now won't be permanent.''

I felt beaten and weakened. I refused to pay for her detective, and I said I wouldn't pay her department store bills, but I knew I would pay them eventually. But no phone bills. No new curtains. She could have the old ones cleaned. I'd see the kids Wednesdays, I told John, and alternate weekends. I'd also spend alternate Sundays and holidays with them. In the main, I gave Janet what she wanted. I consoled myself that I would get a promotion soon that would pay me more money, and the few dollars a week she left me with was only temporary.

One morning at the office, Brenda called me on the intercom. ''Mrs. Edwina Wilson is here to see you. Do you have an appointment with her?''

''Good God, no. Where is she, in the reception room?''

"Yes. Who is she? Why are you so upset?"

"She's my mother-in-law. I knew I'd have to face her sooner or later. Okay, tell the receptionist I'll be right out."

"I could get rid of her if you want," Brenda said.

"She'll just come back again until she gets what she wants, or else she'll make one hell of a scene. Stay put. I'll go get her in a couple of minutes."

When I first met Janet's mother I was very impressed. She was an attractive woman who was always well turned out. Her hair was carefully coiffed, and her clothes were also perfect, never flamboyant. Everything always matched and her jewelry was discreet.

When Edwina Wilson's husband left her she went to work in a local real estate office in Westchester. Her concerned manner, her All-American mother look carefully concealed a will and determination that made her a top salesperson.

After Janet and I married, I discovered that Edwina's guiding star was "They." As in, "They say . . ." or "What do they want?" Her credo was never to do anything that might offend the neighbors. She was banal and bigoted, and during the years that Janet and I were married I did my best to avoid her. When she came to visit, her attention was completely caught by the kids and we had little conversation together.

I waited a few minutes in my office and composed myself, trying to prepare for whatever she might say. I finally went to the reception room to collect her. She looked about ready to cry, but her composure held and we headed toward my office.

I was not prepared for what she did as we passed Brenda's desk. She leaned toward my secretary and said, "You should be ashamed of yourself. I hope you get cancer."

She then turned, marched into my office, and started right in.

"Andy, how could you? How could you leave Janet and your beautiful kids for that tramp outside? I'm mortified. I can imagine what people are saying."

"Do you think I left Janet for my secretary?" I started to laugh.

"Well, didn't you?"

"No, it's not Brenda. There is somebody else, but that's not the whole story. Janet and I haven't been getting along for some time, and it's better for everybody that I left."

Edwina wasn't deterred. She was going to use her selling powers to get me back with Janet. She mentioned the sanctity of marriage, home and hearth, obligations, the inevitable mental breakdown of the children, the shame before the neighbors, the church, and the Bible. She was willing to overlook my peccadillo with another woman: "Forgive and forget, I always say," and finally she tried bribery.

"If it's a matter of money, I'm sure I could help. I have some money I could let you have, and Janet need never know."

I was so outraged I started laughing again. I had to get her out of the office. She tried tears and pleading: "I'm so humiliated—a daughter of mine—abandoned."

I finally got her to the door. The tears suddenly disappeared. She faced me, and her final words were, "You'll be sorry." She marched out, head high, step firm, eyes straight ahead. She passed Brenda's desk and ignored her.

Now that Janet had me tied up financially, she started a campaign on another front: the children.

She called and said, "Andy, I've been worried about Barbara since you left. I've taken her to a psychiatrist."

"When?"

"Last week. He'll be sending you the bill. I talked to him today. He said Barbara has a desperate desire for adult approval. He says if it isn't treated now it could turn into a serious neurosis."

"What did he suggest?"

"He said she needs therapy. It's fifty dollars a visit, and she only has to go once a week."

"Did he think the therapy would take long?"

"I asked him that, but he said he couldn't predict."

"Jesus Christ, where will I get the money? You're getting everything I make already. Why don't you pay the psychiatrist?"

"Me? I can barely make ends meet. Besides, medical bills are your responsibility. If you spent less on *her* you'd have it. It was your decision to leave that upset Barbara in the first place."

I saw no point in arguing. I told Janet I'd think about it. I'd have to borrow the money because Janet was getting it all. Martine was paying practically all our food and household expenses. For my self-respect, Martine let me take her to dinner every other week. I was pinching pennies in a way I hadn't done since I'd put myself through college.

I told Martine that night about Janet's call.

"I'm going to have to borrow the money, and maybe I can talk to Bart about a raise. That or look for a better-paying job."

221

"Andy, you'll find the money. There's no question that Barbara's health is important. It's good to find out now if there's something bothering her. But can I make a suggestion? Why don't you talk to the psychiatrist, too, before she starts therapy?"

That sounded like a good idea. I got the psychiatrist's number from Janet, and called him.

The psychiatrist told me that Barbara was in good shape. Yes, Barbara did seek adult approval, but he believed after talking to her that she had been that way before the breakup. He didn't consider it serious. As a matter of fact, he didn't feel that therapy was really necessary for my daughter. He could talk to her a few times if I or her mother wanted him to, he said, and it might be helpful, but only marginally.

Martine had understood what Janet was trying to do, but couldn't come right out and say it. Barbara's health was at stake, and I couldn't be rational or have any kind of perspective. I was grateful for the calm and skillful way Martine handled the situation and me. I knew it wasn't easy for her. A love affair is a love affair, right? It involves two people, right? Wrong. In our affair there were always Janet and the two girls. Much of my thought and conversation revolved around Janet and the girls. I couldn't help myself, but Martine and I clung to each other and kept insisting that Janet's tactics would not break us apart.

Martine was helpful in so many ways. Tim Bell's apartment was bare and shabby, not really suitable for my children on weekends. I panicked, I couldn't afford to furnish it or even find the time to do it.

"Give me five hundred dollars," Martine said, "and I'll fix up the whole apartment in a week."

"How can you? I need beds, tables, chairs, a new sofa, stuff for the kitchen."

"Don't ask questions, just give me five hundred."

Martine did it. It wasn't right out of Bloomingdale's, but it worked. Martine had found a secondhand furniture store and bought everything I needed. It was bright, even gaudy, but it was serviceable, and if you didn't look too closely, it looked clean. Now I was ready to have my daughters spend weekends with me.

My visiting privileges were Wednesday evenings when I took the kids to dinner, alternate weekends, and alternate Sundays. Wednesday evenings were torture because I had to pick them up precisely on time or Janet would start bitching. I was forced into the position of seeing and being with her. Often she would present me with a new bill, knowing I wouldn't argue in front of the children. I'd accept it, grit my teeth, and know I'd have a fight on my hands the following day. On Wednesdays I'd take the girls to a local restaurant. I always looked for cheap ones where they could eat and I could have a cup of coffee. It was too early in the evening for me to eat dinner, and I preferred having dinner with Martine. Her cooking was excellent and her company soothing. And I needed soothing after being with the girls and seeing Janet. Places like McDonald's were aptly designed for daddies with visiting privileges. McDonald's is not only a family restaurant, it's the perfect split-family restaurant.

But if Wednesday evenings were painful, they were at least brief. Weekends were different.

I was used to taking care of the girls on weekends when Janet and I lived together. But they had their rooms to play in, their toys, and their friends whom they could visit or who visited them. It was a natural setting without too much strain. At my bachelor apartment it was very different. They had to share an unfamiliar bed in the living room, a sofa that opened into a bed, while their daddy slept on a cot in the kitchen. They didn't have their playthings. Their friends were in a different part of town. There was no familiar playground in the area. All they had was their loving daddy who was going to be an unending source of joy and diversion for an entire weekend, from Friday evening to Sunday evening. To prepare the apartment for their first visit I called a maid service out of the Yellow Pages. The cleaning woman showed up at the designated time, and I opened the door to let her in. She looked around the apartment, "Some place you got here, mister. I dunno if I can work here. After all, cleaned Diana Ross's apartment once. Now, that's an apartment!"

I didn't want her to escape. "Well, you're here now, so you might as well do the job."

"I dunno, I guess you're right. But you betta have all the equipment. You got a vacuum cleaner?"

"Not yet. But you won't have to vacuum the rug, it's new, sort of."

She began to retreat towards the door.

"Look, do the best you can. I'm sure you'll do a great job. And if you finish before the end of the day I'll still pay you for the whole day." I began helping her off with her coat.

"Well, all right, but I don't guarantee no perfect job. And, oh yeah, I don't do windows."

The first weekend the girls were to spend with me Janet got suspiciously generous and offered to bring the girls over. I wouldn't have to pick them up, she was going to a dinner party in the Village anyway. At the exact time agreed upon, the doorbell rang, and there they were, suitcases and all. As soon as Janet entered the apartment, her head began to turn as if on a swivel. There was quite a contrast between my secondhand furniture and the apartment I had left behind.

Janet gave me very specific instructions on how to handle the children over the weekend.

"Maybe you've forgotten," I interrupted her, "I took care of the kids every weekend when we were together."

She went right on. "Not too much junk food, and don't let them stay up too late. Maybe you should take them to the playground near our house."

She left after that, and after exploring the small apartment, Barbara asked, "What are we going to do now, Daddy?"

It was a question I would hear from both girls many times that weekend and every weekend thereafter. My routine is familiar to every separated or divorced father.

Breakfast. Supermarketing after breakfast. Visit the Steins after lunch, because they have a son Barbara's age. Dinner. Television. Bedtime, complete with a story or two. Sunday. Breakfast. Television while I straighten up. Playground visit. Lunch. A Walt Disney double feature uptown. The next weekend the Museum of Natural History.

The carousel in Central Park was another favorite with my kids, and I would send them around five times. I used to ride with them, but I would find myself dizzy after the second turn. Then off for an ice cream cone or a box of Cracker Jacks—our favorites.

Visiting my friends who had kids didn't turn out too well. The wives put up with the visits because they felt sorry for the girls, but they didn't approve of me. They would talk to the kids and ignore me, leaving me with a husband forced to keep me company. The men would try not to be too friendly, or their wives would disapprove. Even those friends I thought wouldn't take sides did, and it seemed every tie I had with the past was being cut.

During my weekends with the children I made a startling discovery. They didn't have to eat at a set hour, after all. I found that I could enjoy having meals with them.

We would go to the supermarket and they'd help select the food. It wasn't all cookies and candy as you might expect. They liked milk and hamburgers and pasta, and like their father enjoyed lamb chops and mashed potatoes. We'd walk down the aisles and we'd decide together what we would have for dinner. Back at the apartment they enjoyed helping me. Barbara would stir the spaghetti sauce, and Diane's tiny hands would mold tiny meatballs. If supper was ready at six, we'd eat at six, if it was ready at seven, we'd eat at seven. Then they'd have the dessert of their choice. It was relaxed and fun, and not regimented.

One Sunday evening as I was taking the kids back to their apartment I passed a flower stand. I stopped to buy Martine a bunch of anemones.

"Who are the flowers for, Daddy?" Barbara asked.

"They're for a friend of mine."

"What's your friend's name?"

"Her name's Martine. You'll meet her sometime."

Before there was time for any more questions we were at the door to their apartment building, and I kissed them and sent them upstairs.

The next morning Janet called me at the office. "You bought flowers for Martine last night, didn't you?"

"So what? Are you still having me followed?"

"No. Barbara told me, and she was very upset."

"Why should she be upset about my buying flowers for anybody?"

"Don't you understand? She can't accept another woman in your life. She was upset all evening, and she wouldn't eat her dinner. She cried all night."

"Tell me, when I bring them home do you question them about everything I do or say, or where I go, or who I talk to? If Barbara didn't eat her dinner it was because she didn't like it, or because she didn't like your questions. And I'll buy flowers for Martine whenever I damn please!"

My feelings of guilt had made me agree to wait before I brought Martine and the kids together, and my contact with Martine on the weekends I spent with the girls was limited to phone calls.

Naturally the kids wanted all my attention, and they'd interrupt any phone call with, "Daddy, the TV isn't working," or "Daddy, I'm hungry."

The only time I could talk to Martine was late at night, after the girls had gone to sleep.

One Monday morning I told Brenda, my secretary, how difficult it was keeping my girls happy and occupied during the weekends they spent with me.

"Bring them to my house the next Saturday night

they're with you," Brenda said. "I can cook and I like kids."

I thought it was a great idea, and I was sure the girls would like her. "Just tell me the time, and we'll be there."

"Come as early as you like—come at five. The kids probably like to eat early."

The next Saturday the girls and I went to Brenda's promptly at five. She was great with the girls. No sooner were they introduced than the kids took to her, and she became their instant confidante.

"What did you do today?" Brenda asked.

"Oh, we bugged Daddy," Barbara answered, and they all laughed. I didn't.

Brenda got out a deck of cards and taught the girls the card games she had played as a child. My girls were thoroughly distracted by her, and I could have a drink and relax.

Brenda may have been a good playmate, but she was a rotten cook. She had made a beef and rice dish, and from the looks of the many used pots and pans in the kitchen, she had spent time preparing the dinner. I didn't care if the food wasn't great. The kids liked it, and Brenda was doing a kind thing for me, and I appreciated it.

Brenda and I became friendlier after that. We saw a lot of each other at the office, and when the girls spent weekends with me she would invite us to dinner, or I would ask her to join our excursions to the movies or the museums. Brenda always accepted, and her effervescence and ease with the kids helped make the weekends more pleasant.

I found out a good deal about her personal life, and

she knew about mine. She was my ally in the office, helping field calls from Janet. She knew about Martine, but we didn't talk about her.

My friendship with Brenda cheered me. Most of the people I knew were rallying to Janet's side. Even Jim and my brother thought I had done wrong. It was nice talking to someone who didn't lecture me.

CHAPTER XXIX

Martine

Why, I wonder, do they call it visiting privileges? Andy wanted to see his children, all right—no question about it. But with all the rules and regulations, it seemed more of an obligation than a privilege. There was the obligatory Wednesday night dinner: it couldn't be Monday or Thursday. And then there was the obligatory every-other-weekend routine starting on Friday night for dinner. It could not be Friday *after* dinner, nor could those weekends start on Saturday morning. Friday night for dinner, or else! Or else what, I wondered?

According to Andy, it was follow that routine or the children would pine away, they would be psychologically damaged, their lives ruined. Add to that the obligatory Sundays that alternated with the obligatory weekends, and you can figure out that Andy and I never spent a weekend together.

There were the children looking over our shoulders, the children I had not yet met. We were allowing our relationship to be chipped away by other people. It was afterwards that I understood that Andy was motivated by guilt, and I was too worried about my mother to think straight.

If I had been thinking, I would have told Andy that I wanted to meet his kids. They could have seen that I wasn't the Witch of the West, or the Wicked Queen out of *Snow White*. Maybe they wouldn't have liked me, but I wouldn't be the unknown evil with the silhouette of a monster. An example: Andy told me that Barbara was hysterical after he bought me flowers on Sunday as he was taking his kids home.

The children loomed larger and larger, like the enormous face of the Cheshire Cat seen by Alice, disembodied, but there.

Even my beloved cousin Katy agreed that Janet was right, I shouldn't meet Andy's kids just yet, and a close friend said, "Don't forget, Marty, she is the mother of his children."

I longed for Dee Dee. Longed for her to tell me again that all mothers were not really the Virgin Mary. How had I taken on all the aspects of the Scarlet Woman? In this day and age? Surprising, but true.

Andy came home even heavier with guilt after meeting with the lawyer his brother had recommended. As far as I could see, Andy had agreed to give Janet everything.

"Is that in exchange for a legal separation?" I asked.

"I didn't ask for that," he said, "I've done enough."

232

Done enough . . . been bad enough . . . been cruel enough.

I met Andy's brother, Peter, and his wife, Sally. The four of us went to the theater, and if I was suffering, it was clear that Andy's sister-in-law was wrapped in a cloak of pain, too. Sally and Peter hardly spoke to each other during intermission, and when the four of us left the theater Peter strode on ahead with Andy while Sally and I trailed behind. When we parted, I noticed that Peter was still ten paces ahead of Sally and he didn't notice for a few seconds that she had turned a corner while he continued up the avenue.

I wasn't too surprised a few months later to hear that Peter and Sally had separated.

"My brother said he's learned something from me," Andy told me.

"Yes."

"He isn't giving Sally and his son the same things I'm giving Janet and my kids. He says he knows now you don't have to give that much."

Good for Peter, but for Andy there was no turning back. He finally consulted another lawyer who said that a precedent had been established. John Light had said that the initial agreement would be without prejudice. No such thing, said the second lawyer. If it came to a divorce, Janet would never settle for less, and it was likely she would demand more.

But why should it come to a divorce? Andy and I were drifting apart. We were living together, but everything conspired to separate us. All the world loves a lover? Not true.

Weekends Andy would go off with his children to the small apartment he shared with Tim Bell. Andy would call me in the evening and we'd talk, or try to, but our whispered conversation seemed to wake the kids. I could hear their voices:

"Daddy, who are you talking to?"

"Dad, can I watch TV?"

"Dad . . ."

"Dad . . ."

You couldn't blame Andy's kids. They were trying to hold on to their father, and if Andy, Janet, and I, three supposed grown-ups, didn't know how to handle the situation, what could be expected from two little kids?

What was I doing with the Father of the Year? No, he was more like the Father of the Century, and I was treated again to Katy's cliché: "A good father makes a good husband." I didn't believe that one, and I was beginning to doubt Andy's "Please be patient. Try to understand. Everything will work out."

It was either "Try to understand" or "You don't understand." I was hearing that more and more. And then Peter told me a number of times how fine Janet was, how noble, how good in respect to Andy and his children.

"She's willing to let him see the kids on weekends," Andy's brother said. "Sally never lets me have Mike for a weekend. She's death on visiting privileges."

Poor dumb lady, I thought, remembering the quiet woman who turned down a dark street, away from her husband. If she wanted to make Peter feel guilty and laden with obligation, she should have insisted that he spend every other weekend with their son. That would have shown him!

Was Andy misunderstood by his wife? I was misunderstood by his brother. Andy, sweet innocent, would come home after an evening with Peter, and say, "Peter says I'm so lucky. He says he wishes he could find a woman as intelligent and perceptive as you are."

Intelligent and perceptive. In sex-, youth-, and beauty-oriented America, that's what every woman wants to hear, that she's intelligent and perceptive.

Andy was getting flak from all sides: from Janet, from his kids, from his parents, from Peter, and even from Jim O'Donnell, who probably felt that Andy was setting a bad example to his Ilona.

I was getting flak of a different kind. My friends minded their manners, but every now and then someone asked how could I become involved with a man who had emotional obligations that came before me.

That was the hardest part for me, realizing that I didn't come first with Andy. As an only child I came first to my parents. I married at twenty, and I came first to Davy. Now here I was in third place, sort of an also-ran to the man for whom I had turned my life upside down.

Andy said things that hurt. Like the time he told me that John Light had said that he didn't have to marry me just because we were sleeping together.

"I wish I had a brother," I said.

"A brother? What for?"

"To challenge him to a duel. I don't suppose you'd consider doing that? And if not, maybe you should change lawyers."

Money was also a problem, and that bothered Andy a good deal more than it bothered me. Andy was staying in my apartment, and I didn't feel that we should split the rent. It was the same rent I had always been paying; what difference did it make that two of us now lived in the same space? I felt the same about the other bills, except that Andy would come marketing with me occasionally—possible only on the alternate Saturdays that we spent together—and pay for the groceries.

"You're paying for everything," he'd say, "it's not right."

"Maybe you shouldn't be paying for Janet's new draperies," I said.

Andy was upset. I wasn't living up to that nineteenth-century image of the good mistress. But then, Andy wasn't living up to the nineteenth-century image of the man who kept a mistress.

Why did we stay together? Because there were those moments—those sweet moments that recalled the time—just a few short months before, when we had first met. Some evenings I would fix dinner, we would have it on one of those wonderful bed trays that Andy had bought me, I would turn off the phone, and it would be the two of us, just the two of us, loving and caring for each other.

There were very few times when we could be so unbattered by the rest of the world. That tray I mentioned before? It was one of the few expensive—sixty dollars was expensive for Andy—gifts that Andy gave me. The charged bill went to Janet's address by mistake, and she wrote me a little note:

"I see that Andy bought you a breakfast tray. He bought me one, too, when Barbara was born. Or was it Diane? I forget. I only know he bought me a tray when one of our children was born."

Oh well.

The phone was my nemesis. Andy could never allow a ringing phone to go unanswered, not even if the answering machine was on. I had the theory that if people wanted me, they'd call back, or I could call them at my convenience. But Andy leaped towards a ringing phone. "What if one of the kids is sick? What if they need me?"

Andy had healthy kids, but that didn't stop Janet from using the phone like a guided missile.

"Diane won't eat her peas tonight. And you know how she always loved peas. Remember when we bought a pound of fresh peas on Saturday and she ate them raw?"

"My check is late."

"What about Easter vacation? The kids don't have nursery on Good Friday, so you can pick them up Thursday night."

Visiting privileges, oh my God, visiting privileges. What a privilege.

"Andy should spend more time with you," a friend of mine said, "you should insist. What's that nonsense of their having to sleep at his apartment? Don't they have a home of their own?"

I thought of the new co-op apartment that Andy had bought for Janet, just so that his girls could each have their own room. I almost said, "You don't understand," but I didn't. After all, I didn't understand, either.

If I didn't understand about Andy's children, he didn't understand about my mother. Nor about how I felt, nor how sick she was.

"Why do you persist in thinking that she's going to

die?'' he asked me. "You always go around thinking she's going to die. Not everyone dies of cancer.''

"Not everyone. But a lot of people do. Andy, please—try to remember how you felt when someone you loved was sick—and died.''

"No one I've ever loved has died,'' Andy said.

We both blinked.

"No one?'' I asked.

"My parents are alive. So is my brother. All my aunts and uncles, my friends.''

"You're lucky,'' I said.

"I come from a long-lived family.''

"I don't,'' I said. I thought of my father, of Davy. And now my mother. "That should give you a lot of strength.''

But lack of experience doesn't make anyone strong, and Andy wasn't strong enough to get past his guilt. I wanted to tell him about how guilty I felt—with reason. Guilty because I wasn't spending as much time as I might with my mother. Andy would have plenty of time with his children, a lifetime, but how much time did I have with my mother? Love was separating us. The love we felt for others. My love for my mother, and Andy's love for his children.

CHAPTER XXX

Andy

My parents were upset when Janet and I split up.

"The children. How can you leave the children?"

When I tried to explain how unhappy Janet and I were together, it didn't penetrate or matter.

My relationship with my parents had never been warm or affectionate, but I thought they would be on my side because I was their son. Besides, their relationship to Janet had always been cool and formal—Janet saw to that. Nevertheless, when we split up my parents promptly and squarely placed themselves on Janet's side.

In spite of our stern past relationship, I felt hurt and I stopped calling them. My mother was not to be deterred. She would call me frequently. After one brief question about my health, the conversation took the following form:

"How are the girls?"

"Fine."

"When did you see them last?"

"Last night."

"How were they?"

"Fine."

"How's Janet?"

"Who cares? Flourishing."

"What's new?"

"Nothing much."

"I'd like to hear some news from you."

"Like what?"

"I'd like to hear that you and Janet are back together again. You know it would be best for the kids."

What about what's best for me?

"So long, Ma."

That's why Martine's relationship with her mother seemed so strange to me. When she talked about her mother it was always in loving terms. According to Martine, her mother was never mean to her, never scolded her, was never impatient. Martine would recount stories of her childhood with warmth and nostalgia.

All I could remember of my childhood was the discipline. Martine would tell me glowing stories of her father who had died four years earlier, of his gentleness and understanding, how handsome he was. Well, my father was handsome, too.

Martine would call her mother at least once a day. I'd overhear the conversation occasionally. Martine seemed to embrace her mother through the phone. She'd speak with such tenderness and concern, and she was always offering to do things for her mother—shop for her, cook for her.

"My father is dead," Martine said. "And we have only each other. There is nobody else. I have no brothers or sisters—there's a penalty to being an only child."

The first time I met Martine's mother I was amazed by their affection. They embraced and kissed, and even after the embrace was over they still held on to each other, their arms around each other, or their hands touching. Her mother would talk to me, but she would be touching Martine.

"Isn't she lovely?" she said. "Isn't she wonderful, and so talented."

I agreed with her, even though she didn't have to sell Martine to me. Words of praise from my parents were reserved for great figures like Einstein, da Vinci, and Churchill.

Martine's mother was sick. She was losing weight steadily and the doctors couldn't diagnose her problem at first. Martine spent more and more time with her mother, visiting one doctor after another. She would go to her mother's home and bring her food or prepare meals for her. Since I was living with Martine there was no room for her mother in the apartment. But on weekends when I was with my girls, her mother would stay with Martine. Before I had moved in, Martine's mother would spend several nights in Martine's apartment.

I found Martine's long phone conversations irritating—they intruded on our time—but I never said anything. They mystery of her mother's ailment disturbed Martine, but I tried to reassure her that her mother would recover.

One day Martine told me that she had been given three tickets to the theater and she suggested that we take her mother. I offered to take us all to dinner after the theater. It was a reasonably pleasant evening. I took them to a French restaurant where we discussed the relative merits of the dishes and French cooking in general. After the theater we hailed a taxi and took Martine's mother home.

Soon after that, Martine's mother went to the hospital for a few days. Her latest doctor had advised some tests. Martine asked me to meet her at the hospital after work, and then we would have dinner out.

I had to work late and said I'd meet her after she left the hospital. She agreed, and we chose an inexpensive restaurant in the Village. I had been eager to get out of my loveless marriage, and that eagerness had made me feel guilty. All that, combined with John Light's double-dealing, had left me with much less money than I thought I would have.

It didn't trouble Martine, but it troubled me. I'd talk about my financial plight and Martine would sympathize and then encourage me. She assured me that things would work out. Quietly, she would help. In addition to the rent and the groceries, she paid for the other household expenses. I knew she had eaten out often before I moved in, but now she would encourage us to eat home to avoid the expense. Occasionally I would ask her to go out to dinner, and she'd let me pay the bill in order for me to maintain some pride. We never argued about money, but the knowledge that she was helping support me almost never left my mind. It would lurk shallowly in my subconscious, easily brought out at almost any provocation, such as her being the one to suggest we eat out. My gratitude was heavily larded with resentment, not only towards Janet but towards Martine as well. The resentment wasn't mitigated by a heavy dose of self-pity.

There was a touch of irony in the situation, too. Among other things, Janet had accused me of leaving her for Martine because Martine was rich. I knew Martine was not rich, but I did think she made a good living in a glamorous occupation. After all, she lived in an upper East Side building with doormen, she came and went as she pleased, and didn't keep regular hours like the rest of us. Her articles were published regularly in some of the most popular magazines.

After we started living together I discovered how precarious Martine's occupation really was. Assignments to do an article or story for a magazine were not easy to come by. The competition was fierce, not only from other writers, but from thousands of teachers and housewives and professors who would do anything to see their names in print. They would accept practically no money if their precious article or story were published. Naturally, this abundant and cheap source of material brought the prices down for the professionals and made it harder for them to sell. I read a study Martine had given me, and it said the average professional writer made less than seven thousand dollars a year. Martine made more because she worked hard and developed relationships with a number of magazine editors who knew she could be counted on to deliver their kind of material when they needed it.

Even so, she could have made a lot more money as a copywriter in an ad agency, or working for a public relations firm. But Martine had decided to be a freelance writer, earning less money if necessary, but working on her own. Someday, she told me, she would write a novel or a play.

In spite of the pressures and problems, living with Martine was a new and wonderful experience. I knew that in the flush of a new love affair everything is perfect. But after that first burst of joy and newness is over and the lovers start living together, the seeds of ordinariness, like weeds, crowd in. I was expecting that to some degree and I hoped it wouldn't happen that way with us. It did happen and it didn't.

The daily routine of making a living and coping with others got in our way, but Martine remained an endless source of encouragement and affection. Her belief in me was much more steadfast than mine. She kept telling me how wonderful I was—in and out of bed. She told me she loved me because I made her laugh, and because I was witty and nutty. Martine would tell me how handsome I was; she couldn't understand how Janet and my family had never said that to me. I didn't fully believe that, but I certainly liked hearing it. Even as a teenager, when I was particularly sensitive about my looks, my family and friends used to poke fun about the way I looked, my uneven features, my thick lips. By the time I met Janet I was used to the reality of not being physically attractive to women, so when Janet would poke fun at my looks it didn't bother me too much because I was used to it.

But who doesn't want to be thought handsome? So when Martine would say I was handsome, I liked hearing it and stopped denying it. Martine said that her friends had said the same thing about me. I felt it was Martine's way of being supportive and loyal.

That's another thing I wasn't used to, Martine's loyalty. She was always on my side no matter what happened or what I said. There must have been times when she didn't agree with me, but it seemed as if she did. If Martine had any criticisms, she would couch them so skillfully I never felt I was being put down. If I mentioned a problem I was having at the office we'd discuss it and she would help me find a solution—making me feel as if I had figured it out myself. And more often than not, Martine's solutions worked.

I was always aware of Martine's pride in me and her love for me. And if I forgot, she reminded me. She made me feel I was actually growing. Martine had presented me with a whole new, wonderful, romantic world. Martine and I, with our arms linked, ready to withstand the whole world—we'd not only survive, we'd prevail and win.

How naive can one get? Sure, we loved each other. I loved Martine in a way I had never loved anyone before, but the whole world can be a large and awesome enemy. That cliché, all the world loves a lover, is bullshit.

I found myself arguing with Martine. She would make acerbic remarks about Brenda's devotion to my children and accuse her of other motives. I would defend Brenda. Martine also made remarks about how Janet was running our lives. Christmas that year depressed me, and then Martine wanted me to take her

245

to a New Year's Eve party on a weekend the kids were with me. I didn't want to go, but she insisted.

Martine arranged for a babysitter I felt I couldn't afford, and I went to the party reluctantly. I drank too much, felt miserable, and we had a lousy time. We left early. I dropped Martine at her apartment, went back to mine, paid off the babysitter, and went to bed alone, drunk. Happy New Year!

CHAPTER XXXI

Martine

Christmas came. I had always loved the season. Was it a terribly commercial time? I didn't care. I reveled in the Santa Clauses on the street, the overdone store windows, the tree in Rockefeller Plaza. I didn't know that Christmas would affect my own true love like death.

"Your first Christmas without your children," I heard a well-meaning—well-meaning?—friend—friend?—commiserate with Andy.

"My first Christmas without my children," Andy repeated.

"But you'll see them on Christmas Day," I said, "you'll bring them their presents."

"It's not the same. It's not the same as seeing them wake up and come rushing into the living room for their presents. It's not the same thing at all."

"You want life to be like the cover of an old *Saturday Evening Post* magazine," I said.

"You don't understand."

That again. On Christmas Eve Andy got a call from his brother, Peter, shortly before we left for a party.

"I'm with Janet and the kids," Andy's brother said, "I didn't want you to worry about them on Christmas Eve, you know, being without you, so I came over for dinner. Don't worry, everything's fine."

Andy repeated the conversation and I exploded.

"He's split from his wife and kid, too," I said. "If he's so concerned, why isn't he spending the evening with his son?"

"Because he's in Michigan with Sally and Sally's parents. Listen, I think my brother is doing a darn nice thing, spending the evening with Janet and my kids. He's doing it for me."

The party that night—I can remember nothing about the party, nothing but a sense of heaviness, a wonder at myself, a constant thought: what am I doing here?

On Christmas Day Andy went off to see his children and I went off to visit my mother. My mother, who had always looked slight and elegantly fragile, now looked positively transparent.

"Andy is nice, isn't he?" she prodded me. "He's good-looking, and has a marvelous sense of humor. Does he make you happy, Martine? He does, doesn't he?" My mother's dark brown eyes were feverish.

I knew the answer that she wanted, and I had to give it to her.

"Yes, Mom, he makes me very happy."

She was sitting on the couch when I came into the

house, and now she stretched out. She looked relaxed, relieved.

"I'm so glad, Martine, so glad. That's important to me. I'm sure things will work out for the two of you."

I wasn't at all sure, but I couldn't tell her that.

"How do you feel, Mom?" I didn't wait for an answer. "Do you feel up to going shopping with me next week? They're having a private sale at Bergdorf's."

"I don't need any clothes just now, Martine."

"Of course you do. Once you finish these treatments for that infection that's been bothering you you're going to want to go out again. And you know you can never find anything just when you need it."

My mother brightened. "Do you think I'll need new clothes? I hate to just buy things—"

"Of course you'll need them. Let's go to Bergdorf's on Monday, first thing."

My mother sat up. She looked stronger, better. "All right. If you really think I need new things, Martine."

"I really think so."

"Fine, I'll meet you at Bergdorf's on Monday. Ten o'clock. Besides, I'd like to buy something nice for you, Martine."

"No. Not for me. I have everything. This is for you—I want you to get something."

When we met at Bergdorf's we went to the coat department and I saw that they had a special on a particular kind of reversible coat that my mother had always admired. It was a wool coat faced with another color wool, light, elegant—just my mother's style.

"Look, Mom, here's just the thing. Green on one side—it would be a good color for you—and rose plaid on the other, try it on."

My mother's fingertips brushed against the coat.

"I like the colors. Most double-faced coats are either beige or gray. I've never seen one in such a nice green."

"Try it on. Come on."

"Well," my mother's eyes brightened, new clothes always did that to her. "Well, while I'm here, I may as well try it on."

The coat was a size six, my mother's size, but this coat looked huge on her. The shoulders hung away from her, and the back was much too full. My mother walked to the mirror.

I stood beside her. "I love it. Of course, it has to be shortened. That'll make all the difference."

A saleswoman came over. "That coat is too big—much too big. We don't have it in a smaller size, and this is definitely too big. Your mother? She's very thin, isn't she?"

I looked in the mirror and saw the fright in my mother's eyes.

"I hate skimpy coats," I said. "You'll wear a sweater under it, won't you, Mom? That coat's not too big at all. Just too long, that's what makes you think it's too big. It's a nice coat—it's the coat my mother always wanted."

"But look," the saleswoman said, "just look at the shoulders—"

I stepped in front of her. "It's fine. We'll take it."

The saleswoman shrugged. "I was just trying to help."

My mother stroked the coat's soft fabric as she looked in the mirror. "I'm terribly thin, aren't I? I didn't

250

realize. It's a size six, Marty, and look how it hangs on me."

"That's because it's too long. Could you get a fitter over here?" I asked the saleswoman. "The coat has to be shortened."

The fitter came and quickly pinned up the bottom of the coat.

"There," I said, after the fitter had finished. "Now it looks fine."

"It looks fine," my mother said, "but I look terrible. Look at me."

"Department store lights never do anything good for anyone," I said. "You don't look terrible, and I like that coat on you."

My mother slipped out of the coat and held it to her. She looked at me over the armful of fabric. "Isn't it silly to buy a coat now?" she asked. "The doctor said I may have to go to the hospital for an operation. Just a small one, if the treatments don't work. Don't clear up the infection, I mean."

"That's not sure," I said. "Besides, even if you do go to the hospital, you'll need a coat when you leave the hospital. What has the hospital to do with it?"

My mother turned from me and put the coat on again. She looked at her reflection in the three-way mirror, and we looked into each other's eyes.

"You really think I'll get some use out of this coat, Martine?"

"I'm sure of it. I've never lied to you, have I? Whenever I've told you something looks good on you and you should buy it, you've never been sorry, have you?"

"That's true."

"Fine," I took the coat from her. "I'll charge it to my account, and when the bill comes we can argue about it. I'll have it sent out."

My mother reached out to stroke the fabric. "As long as I'm getting it, I'd like to take it home now. I'll have it shortened in the neighborhood. It takes so long when you have something sent, and this way I can have it right away."

"Good idea. They can pack it up, and we'll take it with us."

"Unless you want to do more shopping," my mother said, "maybe it will be in the way, a big box, and we want to go to lunch, too."

"It won't be in the way. We'll take it with us right now."

My mother smiled, and the terrible transparency seemed to diminish.

"Well, at last," she said, "my double-faced, reversible wool coat. I always said I wanted three things: a coat like this, a black bra, and a pair of snakeskin shoes. I have the coat, and I have the bra, now all that's missing are the shoes."

"We'll look for them here. Maybe we'll be lucky with the shoes the way we were with the coat."

I felt as though the hard knots in my stomach had loosened. It was all nonsense, the idea that my mother could be so ill. There we stood, talking about coats, bras, and shoes. Everything was going to be all right.

"Come on," I said, after the coat was wrapped and handed to me in a silver box, "let's have lunch at the Palm Court and celebrate your new coat."

"We'll go wherever you want," my mother said,

"lunch is on me. But don't you have some work to do? Aren't I keeping you from something?"

"I don't feel like working today," I said. "I'd much rather have a ladylike lunch."

We ate at the Palm Court with the Bergdorf's box occupying a third chair.

"Would you like me to check it for you?" the maitre d' asked.

"No," my mother said. "It's not in our way."

The day after that my mother and I started on another round of seeing doctors.

"Operate," the first doctor said.

"Operate," the second doctor said.

"Operate," the third doctor said, and because I was seeing him without my mother present, he added. "If your mother doesn't have the operation the cancer will completely close off her esophagus, and you'll watch her starve to death. How would you like that?"

I was the one who had to persuade my mother to submit to surgery.

"You too?" she whispered. "You know how I feel about hospitals, operations. Look what happened to your father."

"This is different," I said. "Some operations are a success, Mom, you know that."

"Sure, I know, the operation was a success, but the patient died."

"Not this time."

"Are you sure this is what you want me to do?"

"Yes."

"All right, then."

We consulted again with our family physician, and chose one of the best surgeons in New York. Dr. Matthew Sloan, Chief of Surgery, with framed diplomas all over the walls of his office.

"Shall we say two weeks from today? You'll have to be on the waiting list. New York University Hospital is a big place, but the rooms are still at a premium."

"I can wait," my mother said.

My mother was scheduled to go in to the hospital on Sunday, but we had to wait and see if there was a room available. I took a cab to Riverdale, and my mother and I sat in the living room waiting for the hospital to call.

"Maybe they won't call," my mother said, hopefully.

"You'll be fine after the operation," I said. "it's better to get these things over with."

"Is it? Are you sure?"

"Oh sure, that's what all the doctors have told us. We've seem four of them."

"Yes. Four."

"Mom, do you want something to eat?"

"I'm not hungry. You go ahead, Martine. You have something."

"I'm not hungry, either."

We sat and looked at the phone some more.

"I think I would like a drink, though."

"Yes," my mother said. "Fix me one, too."

We both sipped scotch, neat, and looked at the phone again.

"Maybe there's no room available today," I said, and I felt relief. Cowardly, wonderful relief. A day away from the hospital was a day longer for life.

My mother brightened. "Maybe."

It was three o'clock when the phone rang.

"There's room," I told my mother.

We moved around the apartment. Two ghosts. Are the windows locked? The lights off? Do you have everything?

"Your coat, Mom. Where's your new coat? Don't you want to wear it to the hospital?"

My mother shook her head. "It's being shortened. I'll wear it when I come home."

I called for a cab, and the two of us rode down to New York University Hospital. There was a crowd milling around the lobby and a million forms to fill out.

"Blue Cross? Blue Shield? Major medical?"

"Yes," my mother said, "I have everything."

"Major medical?" I asked. "I didn't know you had major medical, Mom."

"See? You don't know everything about me."

An aide took us upstairs to a private room overlooking the East River.

"It's a nice view," I said.

"I could do without it," my mother said.

I stayed with my mother until eight o'clock, and then I went home to Andy, who said, "Let me tell you what Barbara said, and let me tell you what Diane did. They're going to be fine, Martine. I know they are. I'm always afraid that I'm going to lose them, but no such thing. They love me. No matter what Janet tells them."

"That's nice."

"How are you, babe? How was your day?"

"Andy. I took my mother to the hospital."

"Martine," Andy reached for me. "You've got to forgive me. I can't help myself. I start thinking about

255

my kids, and they push everything else out of my mind, even something more important, like your mother."

That's when I decided it was really over between the two of us. It would always be like this between me and Andy, and I couldn't live that way. I would wait until my mother was out of the hospital. And then I would say goodbye to Andy.

I spent most of the next two days at the hospital while my mother was being tested and re-tested. Why all the tests, I wondered? The doctors knew it was cancer.

"It's for the records," a nurse told me. "This is a teaching hospital."

"Please don't learn on me," my mother said. "I'm not here to be experimented upon."

"Of course not," the nurse said. "That isn't what I meant."

"What did you mean?" my mother said.

"I'll be back later to see how you're doing," the nurse said, retreating out of the room.

My mother got out of bed a little later, and the two of us began to walk to the center of the corridor where there were some stiff, Naughahyde-covered chairs for the patients and their visitors.

As we left my mother's room, a woman from the next room came out into the corridor.

"How are you, today?" she boomed. "Feeling better?"

My mother shrank back and pulled at my sleeve. She looked as though she were staring at death.

"Did you see?" my mother asked as we walked on. "Did you see the sign on that woman's door?"

"What sign?"

"It says, 'Do Not Enter. Infectious.' Did you see that?"

I hadn't seen it. I was too busy concentrating on my mother to look around me. But when I took my mother back to her room, I looked, and there was the sign.

"Isn't that terrible?" my mother asked. "Shouldn't they keep people like that away from people who are being operated on?"

"It's probably nothing serious," I said. "It can't be. It must be something very minor."

"Minor? If it's minor, why would they have that sign on the door?"

And then it was the day before the operation, and I stayed with my mother to the end of visiting hours. Not that the hospital would have minded if I had stayed on longer. Hospitals are like that the night before major surgery.

"Is Andy coming to see me?" my mother asked.

"Yes he is, and then we're going out to dinner with some friends of his."

"Good, I'm glad you're doing that. And I'll see you in the morning before—before—won't I?"

"I'll be here way before they take you down."

I stared out of the window at that marvelous view, and Andy came in. He brought lovely, expensive Swiss chocolates, and he said all the right things to my mother. The chimes sounded, signaling the end of visiting hours, and Andy and I left the hospital.

We met Jill and Roy Fairfax and a business friend of theirs at a nearby restaurant. I had a double scotch, followed by another double scotch, and I began to feel so crazy that the Fairfaxes' friend was sure I was flirting with him. And because today a flirtation ends up in bed, he became aggressively attentive. Andy was talking to Jill, so he missed the other man's wink and comment to Roy, "I feel like riding tonight, boy, and I think I got me a partner."

I moved my chair an inch closer to Andy's and when there was a pause in the conversation, I said, "I'm awfully tired, Andy. Would you mind if we went home?"

The Fairfaxes' friend said, "Hey, I didn't know you two were together."

I could have said We're not, we're pretty far apart, but why complicate things? Andy and I went home.

"Your mother's going to be all right," Andy said, "you'll see, Martine. She's going to be all right."

"Yes."

My mother was operated on the next day, and she went into intensive care after the surgery. She was fragile, but she did seem slightly better each day, or maybe I was seeing her with eyes of hope and my own terrible need.

On Sunday, the fifth day after the operation, I went to see her in the morning, and she was clearly worse. She was speaking in French, and she was delirious. I put my hand on her forehead, and I was sure she had a high fever.

I went to the nurse's station and asked the nurse on duty to look at my mother. I told her about the delirium and the fever.

The nurse shrugged. "Sometimes people get confused after surgery." She walked over to her bed, bent over my mother and shouted, "Lillian. How are you feeling, Lillian?"

My mother didn't answer.

"See," the nurse said, "postsurgical disorientation."

"Even if my mother hadn't been operated on she wouldn't have answered you. She doesn't know you. Please don't call her by her first name. Call her Mrs. Lukas."

The nurse backed away from the bed. "I'm busy right now. She'll come to in a little while."

"But she has a high fever," I said. "Please call Dr. Sloan."

"He was here this morning on his rounds." Her voice was sharp. "You can't expect him to run back here, especially on a Sunday, just because your mother is a little out of it. She's all right on the monitor."

"But the monitor doesn't monitor fever," I said.

"I told you, a lot of patients are like this after surgery." She walked away.

I ran out into the hall and found a telephone. I called my mother's internist, Dr. Adler, and he responded to my description of my mother's symptoms immediately.

"I'll get hold of Sloan and I'll be there in fifteen minutes. Hold on, Marty."

I went back into intensive care—why did they call such lack of care intensive?—and I held my mother's hand. I spoke to her in French, and after a few minutes she opened her eyes. I could see that she knew me.

"Marty," she whispered in English, "what's going to happen to you?"

"I'm going to be fine, Mom, because you're going to be fine. Dr. Adler and Dr. Sloan are on their way. You probably need different medication, that's all."

Both doctors arrived within half an hour, and they confirmed what I knew—my mother had a high fever.

Dr. Adler took me aside. "Something's gone wrong in there, Marty. Sloan is going to have to open her up."

"Not another operation. She isn't strong enough. Can't you do something to bring the fever down first? Maybe she doesn't need another operation."

"Marty," Jim Adler said, "Sloan thinks the stitches may have opened. It could be peritonitis. There's nothing to do but operate, it's the only chance."

I went back to my mother. "Mom," I took my mother's hand, "Dr. Sloan has to take a look at the stitches, just to be on the safe side."

"Marty," my mother gripped my hand, "not another operation."

"No, not exactly."

The nurse who wouldn't call Dr. Sloan handed me a piece of paper. "You'll have to sign this," she said, "permission to operate."

"Marty," my mother said, "Marty."

Knowing that I was betraying my mother, I signed the paper. My mother was transferred to a gurney, and I held her hand as they wheeled her to the elevator.

I couldn't speak, because I wanted to say the unsayable, *Don't die, please don't die. Don't leave me.*

Waiting for the elevator, my mother took my hand and brought it to her lips. "It's all right, Marty," she said, her voice normal and sweet once again, "you're my good child. You're doing the right thing."

The elevator door opened, and my mother was wheeled away.

I sat by myself in a little room away from the larger lounge where patients and their visitors meet. Each floor of the hospital had these little rooms, soundproof

260

and reserved for those who were to hear the ultimate bad news.

My mother was wrong after all. The patient died, but the operation hadn't been a success, either. Dr. Sloan, the best surgeon, explained that he was very sorry, but my mother's death had been caused by a symbiotic infection. It had nothing to do with his skill as a surgeon, he assured me. The stitches had opened, true, and then peritonitis had set in. He had gone in and re-stitched. But he couldn't do anything about that mysterious infection.

"The stitches opened?"

"Your mother was very frail," he said reprovingly, "I think you knew that before we started."

"And what about the infection? What kind was it? There was a woman in the room next door to my mother. There was a sign on her door. It said 'infectious.' And that woman was walking around the hall."

"What woman?" Dr. Sloan asked. "I don't know anything about that. We don't do these things purposely, you know. These things happen. We're not trying to make you unhappy."

Unhappy! I stared at him.

"Now," he said, "we do like to get to the bottom of these things, in the interest of science, you know. Would you give us permission to do an autopsy on your mother?"

That's when I really lost it.

"She's had enough," I screamed in that soundproof room. "Don't touch her. Don't you dare touch her again!"

I don't know what more I might have said if Andy hadn't appeared just then. He came into that small

261

room, brushed past the doctor, and took me in his arms.

"It's okay," he said, and he held me tightly against him. "It's okay."

"No," I said, and I sobbed, "No, it'll never be okay again."

CHAPTER XXXII

Martine

After the funeral Andy said, "I didn't know, Martine, I didn't understand. I'm sorry. I wish I could say that to your mother."

"I know," I said. "There are things I wish I could say to her, too."

A few days later one of my mother's friends came to see me, bringing with her the reversible coat from Bergdorf's.

"Were you shortening it for my mother?" I asked.

"I was just holding it, Martine. Your mother didn't want to shorten it. She said this way it would be just the right length for you."

When Andy came home that night he found me sitting in the dark in the living room, wrapped in the reversible coat.

"Martine, I'm going to take you away this weekend. Okay? I'll find us a nice place."

263

"How can we go away? What about Barbara, what about Diane? Isn't this your weekend with the kids?"

"Don't worry about it. I'll figure something out. I'm taking you away, Martine."

And Andy did just that. We stayed in a hotel on the ocean, and we walked on the beach and talked and drank and made love, and I cried and Andy cried, and we told each other how we would never let anything come between us, not anything, not ever.

Sunday night when we came home we walked into the apartment to the jangling of the telephone. Andy answered it, and I walked into the other room, but I heard him.

"Don't cry, Barbara. Of course I love you. Hi, Diane honey. How's my baby? I had to, girls, I just had to. Somewhere, just somewhere. It couldn't be helped. It was something I just had to do . . .

"Damn it, Janet, don't scream at me! Of course I love my kids. What a stupid question. All right, I'll make it up to them. I'll take them for the next two weekends."

I walked into the kitchen. I took the coffee cups out of the cabinet and I threw them one at a time at the wall until they all lay in shards on the floor.

Andy heard the noise. He hung up the phone and came into the kitchen.

"You shouldn't have done that, Martine," he said. "You liked those cups. And if you had to throw them, I wish you had thrown them at me. Not at the wall."

"Would that have made you feel better?"

"Yes."

"Sorry."

"I'm the one who's sorry," Andy said, "I'm just

beginning to understand myself. Marty, I'm being torn apart. I can't live with you, I can't live with anyone."

"Except your kids."

"Except my kids."

I wasn't angry. I was exhausted. "Andy," I said, "you can't devote your life to your kids. That's crazy."

It was inane, the way I kept repeating myself, but I felt as though I was talking to a lunatic.

"Are you going back to Janet?"

"No! You showed me what it was like to live with a loving woman, I would never go back to her."

"I'm glad I showed you," I said. "A lot of good it's done the both of us."

"I'm sorry, Martine."

For the next few days we were so polite to each other it was disgusting.

"I'm sorry."

"No, I'm sorry."

"But it was my fault."

Andy stayed in my apartment while he looked around for a place that would be better for him than Tim Bell's apartment. This was the ending I had been waiting for on Labor Day. It was happening months later, and it was much worse.

It was while all this was going on that my friend Phyllis arrived from her place in Newport on her way to her apartment in Mexico City.

"Martine, you look terrible. I'm sorry about your mother, I know how close you were. I'm glad you've got Andy, though. I'd hate to think of you all alone."

"Andy and I are splitting up. It's all over."

"Don't tell me the details," Phyllis said, "you'll just suffer more if you have to repeat them. You better come down to Mexico, Martine. I'll go down and open the apartment, and it'll be all ready when you get down. Today's Monday. How about Saturday? I'll meet you at the airport.''

"I don't know—"

"That's all right, I do. Saturday, I'll be expecting you. Let's call Eastern right now and make a reservation.''

"But—"

"Never mind, I'll do it,'' and she did.

After her call to Eastern, Phyllis left. "I don't want to see Andy,'' she said. "I'll kill him if I do.''

"Phyllis—"

"Never mind. I don't want to hear about it. Don't say goodbye, Martine. I'll see you in a few days. Saturday, Mexico City, Martine.''

Before I left New York Dee Dee called and asked me to come to California, but then she said, "How could you let your mother be operated on, Martine? You always said you didn't trust hospitals or doctors. How could you let them do that to her?''

I couldn't bear to explain the grim story of the alternative to the operation, but I kept hearing Dee Dee's question, the same question I asked myself, and I decided I'd rather be with Phyllis who didn't want to hear unhappy details about anything.

Phyllis was right. I'd go to Mexico. Andy could stay in my apartment until he found another place. By the time I came back he'd be gone and I could go on with life once again.

Andy and I said goodbye on Friday morning. It was his weekend with the children.

"I'm sorry I can't take you to the airport tomorrow," he said, "but the kids—"

Andy hadn't asked me where I was going, but he assumed I was going to California.

"I know Dee Dee will be glad to see you."

I didn't answer. Didn't bother explaining that I was going to Mexico. What difference did it make? He didn't care where I went, as long as I left him alone.

We said goodbye again, and just because I wanted to, I threw my arms around him and gave him a hug. It was over, but at least he would remember me the way I once was, not the frozen person he had turned me into.

There was the hug, and then Andy was walking, no, almost running, down the hall, and I slammed the door behind him. And I mean really slammed it.

"I don't understand you," my cousin Katy said, when I called to say goodbye. "If you love Andy, how can you leave him?"

"Goodbye, Katy."

"I love you, Marty, but I've never understood you. You're the family eccentric. That's what everybody says."

Except my mother, she didn't think I was the family eccentric. Goodbye, goodbye Andy, goodbye Katy, goodbye everyone.

CHAPTER XXXIII

Andy

Martine and I broke up.

I had done it. The best thing that ever happened to me just slipped away from me because I couldn't handle the pressures. I had expected Janet's assaults, but I hadn't expected my family to align themselves on Janet's side because of the kids. But that's what they did, all of them.

My friends, such as they were, abandoned me. Except for one of them, Hal Green, I didn't mind. They were Janet's friends, anyway.

The worst of it was that I couldn't help Martine with her mother. When she needed my support I wasn't there.

I'm not a religious man, but I knew God was testing me and I had failed. He had shown me true passion and emotion for life and death and I wasn't ready to accept.

What I seemed to want was an uncomplicated life and I got it.

I moved my things out of Martine's apartment into my tenement flat. My commitment would be to my kids.

CHAPTER XXXIV

Martine

Phyllis met me at Mexico City Airport in her usual style: with three cars and twenty-one people, two of whom were musicians who had brought their guitars to escort me from the airport to the parking lot. Then there were two smiling girls—sisters, I learned—who gave me armloads of carnations.

"Phyllis," I asked, when I was seated in one of the cars, "who are all these people?"

"My friends and your friends, too. This is Ana and Maria, and that's Jose, Luis, Ricardo, Javier. Oh, never mind, you'll meet them back at the house. They're all coming to the house for a drink."

I was tired, exhausted, unhappy. I didn't want to sit around with a bunch of people I didn't know. I wanted to lie down in a darkened room and weep. But there was no use saying that to Phyllis.

Phyllis was not going to let me weep, she was going

to see to it that I was amused, distracted, and continuously busy. My weeping times were restricted to mornings, when over breakfast I would tell Phyllis the saga of my months with Andy Lang.

Phyllis was a sympathetic audience—until ten-thirty each morning, when the phone would begin ringing and the day would commence with an auto trip to the provinces to see a young *novillero* fight his first bull, or a drive to someone's ranch to see a *tienta*—a testing of the progeny of the brave bulls—or a pre-luncheon meeting to decide who was going in who's car the coming Sunday to the Plaza Mexico to see that day's *fiesta brava*.

Say *bullfight* to most North Americans and they groan, sneer, or make strange noises signifying disgust. Thanks to Phyllis and her involvement with the taurean world of Mexico, I will never behave in such a provincial manner.

I learned about the art of bullfighting and its history. It was considered much more than a sport in Mexico. It was also more than an art; for true aficionados like Phyllis, it was a religion. I also promise to wrestle any *Norte Americano* to the ground who, when told that bullfighting is dangerous, says, "Yes, for the bull." Don't say that to me, sir, as you eat that double-thick sirloin steak.

Because Phyllis kept open house—the closest I've ever come to the European idea of a *salon*—I met many of Mexico's matadors. They would stop by in the afternoon for a coffee, or in the evening for a brandy. They were normal, friendly, often amusing, and no more *macho* than the average man you'll meet on a busy night at Maxwell's Plum. Indeed, they were a relief

om the New York men Dee Dee and I had been
eeting during the past few years. It was simple. The
ouble standard was still the rule in Mexico. If you
id, you were one kind of woman, and if you didn't
ou were another kind—and eligible to be a friend and
ompanion.

I'm not saying that Mexican men didn't try to tempt
ou from being a woman who didn't to a woman who
id, but while they tried they didn't insist. And they
arely pouted or acted hurt if you said no.

There was one handsome matador who did get a
ttle edgy when I said no, and the next time we met
t a party he said, "You won't like this party—too
any Mexicans."

I waited until he next came to Phyllis's and I greeted
im with, "You won't like it here—too many Ameri-
ans."

He laughed, apologized, and we became friends.
uch good friends that Phyllis became worried.

"Don't get involved with a Mexican man," she cau-
oned, "they're great as friends, terrible as hus-
ands."

"Husbands! I wasn't thinking of that."

"Well, *I* was thinking—strange things happen when
ou're on the rebound."

I didn't answer. I was having a good time—I felt I
ad been transported to an exotic society where the
atives were certainly friendly. I was really not re-
ounding. I went to sleep thinking of Andy, and I woke
p thinking of Andy, and one morning when I looked
t Phyllis across the coffee cups, I realized I had told
er the story of our breakup every morning for three
veeks.

"I'm a bore," I said.

"Oh no—no." And then, "Yes. But not to me, Martine, just to yourself. He's not worth all this—all this agonizing, all this repetition of what he said and you said.

"Who cares? You shouldn't. Let him go enjoy his life with his children if that's what he wants. He doesn't appreciate you. Forget him."

"You're right, I know your right. You'll see, I'm not going to talk about him, not ever again."

But the next morning over breakfast, my whole litany started once again. Phyllis was patient. She was more than patient—she was kind and loving, but one day she did explode.

"I could kill him, this Andy Lang of yours. He has no right to make you unhappy. What's wrong with the man?"

"He was depressed, Phyl. Mixed up—a bad case of guilt."

"Depressed? Depressed! Fine, let him go be depressed in a corner all by himself—not in the middle of the living room rug, where everybody can see him and pity him."

"I don't think he wanted pity."

"Why should he? He has so much self-pity he doesn't need anyone else's."

Once again I swore not to talk about Andy to Phyllis, and I kept my vow the next morning at breakfast. And then something happened during the afternoon that made me break down.

The doorbell rang, and when I answered it, a man introduced himself:

"How do you do? I am Jorge Blanco, the maestro the guitar."

"What?"

"Perhaps I did not say that right. The maestro of e guitar. I have come to play for you."

"Phyllis," I called out, "Phyllis—"

Phyllis appeared from her bedroom. "Jorge, how e you? Please come in. This is my friend, Señorita [artine. Martine, Jorge has come to play the guitar r you."

"Of course."

Only in Mexico, and maybe only at Phyllis's house Mexico, would a man arrive at the door to play e guitar and sing. Not for money, but just for the ve of music and the idea of pleasing a friend's est.

I sat back, expecting something pleasant but ama- urish. But a few minutes later I sat up straight. Jorge lanco was no amateur, he was a fine guitarist and an en better singer.

"Phyllis," I said when he was between songs, "Se- or Jorge—you're wonderful—marvelous."

His smile was sweet and shy, and he sipped some of e brandy Phyllis had put beside him.

"Do you play in a theater?" I asked. "A night- ub?"

Maestro Jorge concentrated on his brandy glass.

"He could," Phyllis said, "but he's too shy. He ecomes absolutely terrified when he has to play be- re a group. He's tried—nightclub owners would hire im in a minute—but when he's on stage he freezes. o now he plays for friends, gives guitar lessons, and aakes a living as a civil servant—he works in one of

275

those big offices that have something to do with soci
security."

"What a shame," I said.

"Why?" Phyllis asked. "He's happy and he love
his music. Not everyone has to be a star, Martine. It
only up north that people put so much emphasis o
money and success."

"You're right," I said. "Please play some mor
Maestro."

Jorge Blanco cleared his throat. "This is a song b
Agustín Lara. You know Lara? Olga Guillot made th
song a success, perhaps you have heard it— '*No Me O
vides.*'"

"No, I don't know it."

And then Maestro Jorge showed what a master h
truly was. I understood maybe one word out of five
but the feeling of the song was transmitted through h
guitar and his voice. *Never forget me—No me olvides.* I wi
remember your mouth, I will remember your kisse
and you will never forget me . . .

I started to cry; sentimental idiot that I am, I sa
there weeping. Jorge continued the song until the enc
I imagine he had moved others to tears with that sam
song, but I felt a fool nevertheless, especially foolis
because I was weeping for a man who hadn't loved m
enough to hold onto me.

"It is Señorita Martine's mother," Phyllis explaine
when the song was finished, "she died a short whil
ago, and my friend is sad."

"*Seguro,*" Jorge Blanco said, "losing one's mother i
very hard, most sad."

"One's mother is the only person worth cryin

out," Phyllis said, "other people are quite unimportant."

"You're right," I said, crying even harder, "I know you're right."

Phyllis sighed, "Please play something else, Maestro, Something *alegría*—something to make my friend stop crying."

Jorge Blanco played the happy song Phyllis had requested, and I was able to stop crying.

"You must think I'm an idiot," I said after the Maestro had left.

"I think it's wonderful that you can love that deeply. After Davy died your mother and I worried that you'd ever love anyone again—not ever. I just wish that when you did fall in love, it was with someone who was worth all that caring."

"It doesn't work that way."

"I can see that."

Phyllis was wonderful, all her friends were wonderful. I had never been treated with such kind and loving attention. No one seemed to work, or, at least, they were not on the rigid schedules that were part of life in New York. Someone was always available to join us for dinner at two in the afternoon, or ready to go to hear the mariachi bands in Garibaldi Square, or to take a ride out to the pyramids. There were parties every night, and the big day was Sunday when we went in a large group to Plaza Mexico to see the *corrida*. If a friend of Phyllis's was fighting that day, we'd leave the house early and stop at the hotel suite where the matador was surrounded by his entourage who dressed him in his suit of lights.

It was different and distracting, but every now and

then, more now than then, I would think how And
would enjoy meeting these new people, seeing Mex
ico, observing the taurean world. And when Dee De
called and asked me to come to Los Angeles, I wa
smiling.

"You must be running out of money," Dee De
said, in her typical Dee Dee way. "If you come to L
Angeles I could introduce you to a few people in TV
You might get some work. Look, I know Phyl. Yo
can't tell me that she's thinking of finding you assign
ments in Mexico."

"Phyllis doesn't believe in work."

"Wonderful, as long as your mother's insuranc
holds out."

"There wasn't any insurance," I told her, "any
way, just enough to cover the hospital bills."

"So?"

"I don't know."

"Look," Dee Dee said, "I'm sorry about what
said. I mean about you letting your mother be operate
on. That was dumb. I know there wasn't anything els
you could have done. That's why you didn't come t
L.A. in the first place, right?"

"Right."

"Okay, so I say dumb things. So do you. So doe
everybody. But if I'm your friend, you're not goin
to hold it against me for the rest of my life, ar
you?"

"No. You're right."

"Okay, so when are you coming?"

"Next week," I said, "I'll call you and let you know
the flight number."

Phyllis sighed when I told her that I would be leaving Mexico. "Aren't you having a good time here?"

"Wonderful. But I really ought to think about getting back to work."

"Work. Why does that have to ruin everything?"

I couldn't explain to Phyllis, but for me work would be more of a distraction than constant play.

CHAPTER XXXV

Andy

I didn't announce my breakup with Martine to anyone except Peter. I called and asked him to have dinner with me.

"What happened between you and Janet?" he asked. "It was Martine, wasn't it?"

"I suppose so, but that's not the whole story."

"What's the whole story?"

"Janet and I weren't happy together. That's why I found another woman."

"You mean Martine was better in bed, and you put a romantic halo around it."

"I'm telling you it wasn't that. We were great together in the sack. Better than with anyone else, ever. But I thought there was more."

"What do you mean, thought?"

"We broke up. Martine's left town."

"Good. Then you can come to your senses and g
back to Janet and the kids."

"You're not listening. Janet and I are finished fo
good."

"Did you think Martine was going to be any better
Don't delude yourself with romantic notions abou
love. Love is books and movies. Forget 'they got mar
ried and lived happily ever after.' Ever after is babie:
diapers, bills, plumbers, furniture, fur coats, and mor
bills. And hair curlers. That's ever after. But you'r
forgetting a few people. Your kids. You owe them."

"I know my responsibilities, and I'll handle them
You act as though I'm abandoning my kids and you'v
got to become a surrogate father because I'm such
rat. But the kids are going to be just fine. I'm not goin
back to Janet or anybody. Maybe I was destined t
live alone."

"Okay, okay, let's drop the subject. How do yo
like living alone? Seeing any action?"

Jim O'Donnell was also ready to revel in my new
found bachelorhood. Now he had a drinking buddy
he knew half the bartenders in town, and he had
buddy to make the singles bar scene with.

"Why don't we find us a couple of girls and part
in your apartment?" he kept asking.

"Maybe another time."

And then I went home to my empty apartment.

CHAPTER XXXVI

Martine

Dee Dee was waiting for me at Los Angeles Airport with a chauffered limousine.

"Dee Dee, you didn't have to—a car and a driver, my God!"

"It belongs to this friend of mine," Dee Dee said. "He wanted me to use it. He insisted I meet you with his car."

I looked at Dee Dee. She seemed different. And there had been no sneer in her voice when she had said "this friend of mine."

"Dee Dee?"

"Martine, this is it. I mean, really. Wait until you meet him. He's so terrific, I can't believe it."

If Phyllis had to listen to my sad tale about Andy Lang for hours on end, I had to listen to Dee Dee's happy story about Win Clinton all during the drive to her apartment in Beverly Hills. Win was a lawyer involved with the studio with whom Dee Dee had just signed a huge contract.

"I never felt like this before," Dee Dee said. "And he says the same thing. We looked at each other and *wham*. Martine, he says I'm the greatest talent he's ever met. I told him about this musical I want to write, and he says he knows I can do it. And he wants to back me."

"Dee Dee, that's wonderful."

"The only thing is," Dee Dee hesitated, "he wants to get married."

"Terrific! Why didn't you tell me you wanted me to come to L.A. to be your maid of honor?"

"The only other thing is—he's married."

"Oh."

"But he wants to get a divorce."

"Fine. So he'll get a divorce, and you'll get married and live happily ever after. I love happy endings."

"I don't know," Dee Dee said, "I'm not into this marriage shit. You know that, Martine. I don't want to be somebody's wife, running a house, entertaining, playing that whole shit role—"

"Dee Dee, do you love Win?"

"I'm crazy about him."

"Then marry him. Marriage doesn't have to be a role, something phony. It can be wonderful. It was once with me. Since when do you let other people make definitions that apply to you?"

"Yeah, you're right, I guess." Dee Dee was silent for a few seconds, and then, "Martine, just wait until you meet him!"

I didn't have long to wait. Win Clinton came over

a few hours later and it was clear that he was as much enamored of Dee Dee as she was of him.

"Isn't she wonderful?" he asked, when Dee Dee had left the room. "I'm telling you, she's wonderful. So bright, so talented. I'm going to see to it that she gets to write the kind of music she wants to write. Not all this movie junk. I want to marry her. I guess she told you that."

"She told me," I said. "I'm happy for both of you."

"I have to tell my wife, and that won't be easy. My wife had a slight heart attack a year ago. She's not supposed to be upset. And then there are my kids."

I felt as though I was watching a rerun of a bad soap opera.

"Dee Dee didn't tell me anything about that," I said.

"My kids will be all right. I have a girl eighteen, a boy twenty. But my wife."

I sighed.

"But she'll have to understand, that's all. I want to live out the rest of my life with Dee Dee."

Oh, where did I hear all that before? But Win Clinton seemed stronger, more sure of himself than Andy. He had a reputation of being one of Hollywood's tough guys, a hatchet man in the world of finance and business.

I knew his reputation, but I liked him in spite of it. He was warm and sweet to Dee Dee, gazing at her as if she were some rare, wonderful being, and because I was Dee Dee's friend, he was also warm and sweet to me.

I spent the next few weeks with Dee Dee and Win. They did their best for me, introducing me to TV producers, telling everyone what a great writer I was. But I had no illusions about my making it in Hollywood.

I was always asked two questions: "You got any screen credits? How about TV?"

"No. Just magazine stuff and one book."

"Oh."

And then, "Look we could talk about it, how about coming over to my place after dinner. I got a great little house in the Canyon. How about it?"

"No."

One night Dee Dee and Win took me to one of those parties I'd read about. It was at a producer's home, complete with a kidney-shaped swimming pool that meandered halfway into the living room, and a private movie theater. This was in addition to the rest of the house which looked more like a movie set than a home people lived in.

I gasped when Dee Dee, Win, and I walked into the living room. There were about thirty girls there, each a beauty. No one famous, mind, but each had perfect teeth, hair, eyes, and figure. They possessed all the qualities of a film or TV star, and yet not one of them was even slightly familiar.

"My God, Dee Dee, I'm going home. I feel faded and a hundred years old. Look at these girls. Why do those men you introduced me to make a pass when there's all this around? Were they trying to be polite? I don't get it."

Dee Dee looked around the room. "White bread, Martine, that's all it is, nothing but white bread."

"Right," Win agreed. "And those guys, they're nothing but apples and oranges. Maybe a few bananas thrown in. That's all they are."

286

That was the way Dee Dee and Win spoke of most of the Hollywood crowd: the girls were white bread, the men were apples and oranges with a few bananas thrown in.

Win was so powerful that he could dismiss most of the men he knew just that way. And he was also powerful enough to get Dee Dee a good, annual six-figure contract for two years.

"That's marvelous," I said, when Win told me the news.

"I want Dee Dee to be taken care of," Win said, "always."

"I'm sure you're going to take care of her always," I said.

He didn't answer, and I thought I read the look on his face. *The wife and the kids* . . . I knew that look well. But it wasn't only Win's wife that complicated matters. Dee Dee added her share to his problem.

I was in my bedroom, and they had come in from a party. Their voices carried through the apartment. "Forget it," I heard her scream at Win. "I don't want to marry you."

"But Dee Dee, I love you. You love me."

"Love isn't enough. I can't stand all this shit. I don't want to hear it again. All that stuff about your wife, your kids, what they'll think at your law firm, what they'll say at the studio. I don't want to hear it. Forget it, just forget it!"

I didn't hear Win's answer, if he made any, but I did hear the door slam, and then Dee Dee came bursting into my room.

"It's finished. It's over." Her short blonde hair was

287

a mess, and her eyes looked crazy. "I just can't stand it anymore."

"But you love Win."

"You too, with that love shit! Sure, I love him, but I don't want to hear all his problems. His wife, his kids, and now he tells me that they're going to be upset at the studio if he gets a divorce. Imagine anyone being upset in Hollywood over a divorce! Who cares? I don't. It's interfering with my work. That's what's important—my work."

"Dee Dee. Win is important to you, too."

A few hours later I heard her at the piano, and I recognized a melody from the folk opera she was writing. Was that the answer for me, too? Work? Maybe. Andy had his kids, I would concentrate on writing that book I had said I would do. I fell asleep with Dee Dee's music, alternately plaintive and raucous, threading its way through my dreams. I dreamt about my mother, and when I woke, my pillow was soaking wet. I had been weeping. My mother had looked so sad in my dream—sad and accusing.

The next day Win asked me to have lunch with him, and I listened to an entire monologue of his problems. "Dee Dee doesn't understand. I love her so much, Martine, I'm just trying to figure out the best way we can have a life together."

"Sure, everyone at the studio gets divorced. But I'm not a producer or a director or God forbid, an actor. I'm a corporation counselor, and they're making little cracks about me and Dee Dee. Don't get involved, don't forget your poor sick wife and your two gorgeous kids. It would be okay if I didn't want to marry Dee Dee, but I do, and now those apples and oranges at the studio are saying that Dee Dee would spoil my image. Can you imagine that? They know my wife would drag me through the courts. It would be a mess. But I don't care about that. I just want Dee Dee—I want to make her happy.''

I didn't say anything; I didn't think Win expected me to.

"But it's okay, Martine, I think I've found a way out. I haven't even told Dee Dee yet, but there's a chance that I might get an appointment as a judge. It's been mentioned to me before. The hell with the studio. The wife of Judge Clinton, do you think Dee Dee would like that?''

"Win, you mean it's okay to be divorced as a judge, but not as a corporation counselor?''

"Sure, once you're a judge who can touch you? Nobody. It's crazy, but that's how it is.''

Win wasn't prepared for Dee Dee's reaction and neither was I. She came home that night in a temper.

"The wife of a judge,'' she yelled. "Can you imagine that? Me, the wife of a judge—how boring can you get? Did you ever hear such shit?''

"What difference does it makes what Win does? The important thing is to be together.''

"Martine, grow up. Stop all that junk. I couldn't make it as the wife of a judge—that's not my life. It never will be.''

"Did you tell that to Win?''

"I told him. He's going to Chicago for a few days on business, and he said he's going to think some more. We'll talk when he gets back.''

"He'll think of something.''

I tried to go back to sleep, but I kept thinking, poor

Win, poor Martine, poor everybody. Maybe Andy had the answer for all of us. Don't get involved, it never works out.

The next day, Sunday, Win called from Chicago.

"I'm sorry," I told him, "Dee Dee isn't here. Do you want her to call you back?"

"No, that's okay, I really wanted to talk to you, Martine. I wanted to tell you how happy I am that Dee Dee has you for a friend. It makes me feel good just knowing that."

"Win, do you want me to give Dee Dee a message? Do you want her to call you back?"

"No, I'm going to be in and out. Just tell her I love her, and that everything will work out."

"I'll tell her, Win. I'm glad."

I told Dee Dee when she returned home that Win had called, and I gave her his message. She was in a calmer mood.

"He really is a great guy, isn't he, Martine? I hope he's right. I hope he can work things out."

"I'm sure he can."

It was some time in the middle of the night when I heard Dee Dee scream and scream. I ran into her room, where she was clutching the phone, wailing and saying, "It's not true. It's not true. You're lying to me."

I pulled the phone from her hand. "Who is this? What's happened?"

I heard the news from a studio executive. Win Clinton was dead. There had been a fire. No, not in the entire hotel. Just in his room. He had probably gone to sleep with a cigarette. Strange, though, the police who called said he had made a little bonfire in the

290
290

wastebasket of all the papers and pictures he carried in his wallet. Why would he do that? He must have been drinking.

That's what the man on the phone said, but I knew that's not what had happened. Win had called to say goodbye, he had wanted me to give Dee Dee his final message of love. Win, the tough guy, was no stronger than Andy. Each said goodbye in his own way.

I hung up and Dee Dee clutched me. "He killed himself because of what I said, because I said I wouldn't marry him. That's why he did it. Martine . . ."

I held on to Dee Dee. "It was an accident. A terrible, tragic accident. Win did *not* kill himself. He wasn't that kind of a man. He was looking forward to coming back and being with you, Dee Dee. A man like that doesn't kill himself."

"Are you sure?" Dee Dee was weeping.

"I'm sure."

For the next few days I repeated that message to Dee Dee a dozen or more times. Dee Dee went completely to pieces. A doctor came in every day to sedate her.

"Don't leave me, Martine," she said. "You're my only friend out here. Don't leave me."

"I won't leave you, Dee Dee, I'll stay as long as you need me."

Representatives from Win's studio and law firm came to the apartment. There were papers that Dee Dee had to sign. Win's legacy to Dee Dee was the contract he had drawn up for her. The studio would have loved to break it, but Win had made sure that they couldn't. Dee Dee got her first year's payment in advance. The check was handed to me in the studio's offices by one of Win's assistants.

"That's that," he said. "Win must have really loved that girl."

"He did love her," I said. "It's a tragedy that they couldn't have had a life together."

"It's a tragedy that he died, a tragedy for his wife and kids—that's the tragedy."

I put the check in my bag and started to leave.

"The funeral is day after tomorrow," Win's assistant said. "We'd appreciate it if you'd see to it that she doesn't go."

I saw to it by promising Dee Dee that I would go to the funeral and report back to her.

"I should go too," she wept, "I should say goodbye to Win."

"That's not Win any more, and the doctor said he doesn't want you to go. Win wouldn't want you to go, Dee Dee, he loved you. He wouldn't want you to suffer unnecessarily."

"Don't say he loved me," she screamed, "Say he *loves* me. Somewhere he still exists. Somewhere he still loves me."

"You're right. He does love you. And that's why he wouldn't want you to be there."

The doctor helped me persuade Dee Dee that it would be wrong for her to go to Win's funeral and I went by myself, sitting in the last row of the church. A few people turned to stare and whisper, but it was obvious that I wasn't Dee Dee, and I hadn't been in Hollywood long enough for most people to make the connection between us. I saw Win's wife and son and daughter. They seemed sad.

Poor Win, poor Dee Dee, poor Andy. They reminded me of each other. The minister droned on

292

about what a great husband Win had been, a devoted father, a pillar of the community. Yes, he actually said all those things. I guess it was important to Win to be thought about that way. That's what Win, Dee Dee, and Andy had in common. Their careers, and what other people thought of them were more important than happiness.

Did I know how to be happy? I had been happy once with Davy, but so many years had passed that maybe I, too, had lost the knack. Poor Win. Poor Dee Dee. Poor Andy. And poor Martine.

CHAPTER XXXVII

Andy

My life went on pretty much as I had arranged it. I had my job, I saw the kids. I watched a lot of television, and went to the movies by myself. I had gotten a raise, and my financial problems were eased a little.

I had exactly what I wanted: peace, quiet, serenity. And I felt nothing. Then a new idea of what I should do came to me. I wondered: what was the best and quickest way to kill myself?

What did I want, I literally shrieked one night. I found myself crying. I was alone in my apartment, and there was nobody to see me, so I didn't have to feel embarrassed, but I quickly dried my tears as if someone were watching and tried to compose myself.

What was the matter with me? Didn't I have everything I wanted? The answer was there, and I kept pushing it away, but it wouldn't be stopped. So I finally let it out. I missed Martine. I wanted her back.

Please God, bring her back. I know I ruined the best thing that ever happened to me, but I'll be different if she returns.

I missed the sharing, the laughing at something that tickled us, the having somebody to nudge in the ribs at the movies. I loved the way we shared each other's food in restaurants. Not just to be able to taste each other's dish, but to give nourishment.

I missed the times we would reach a special passage in a book or newspaper and read it aloud. I had always been a secret television watcher. I thought it was the world's greatest invention. When I lived with Janet she used to ridicule me for watching that garbage, as she called it. But Martine loved television as I did. Often, we would lie in bed and watch television all night.

She would bring dinner to the bedroom on a tray and we would watch uninterruptedly from our bed. Martine didn't understand the first thing about baseball or boxing or football. But if I wanted to watch a game on a Sunday afternoon, she would lie next to me with her head on my shoulder, purring, content to be near me and not caring who won or lost or who hit a home run, or who knocked whom out, or who scored a touchdown. She just liked being near me and I liked having her near me. She would say she loved football because she had me close for hours at a time.

I remembered one Saturday evening Martine and I had decided to stay home and I said I would prepare dinner. I cooked one of my favorite dishes, and one Martine had never eaten before, oxtail stew. It didn't sound too appealing, she admitted, but she was willing to try it, and she would help me prepare it. She would be my sous chef. There was a movie on television that we both wanted to see, an old one called *Saratoga Trunk*, starring Gary Cooper and Ingrid Bergman. So we prepared dinner and watched television simultaneously. During commercial breaks we would dash into the kitchen, peel and cut vegetables, prepare the bouquet garni, brown the vegetables, flour the meat and brown it, batch by batch. Back and forth. This was one time we appreciated all the commercials because it gave us the time to prepare dinner without missing the movie. Naturally, it slowed the preparation, but the stew was cooked before the last exciting half hour of the movie, and we ate with our eyes glued to the set. The stew was delicious, Gary Cooper beat up his enemies, and Ingrid Bergman won her man. It was a happy and victorious evening for all, and *Saratoga Trunk* had become our all-time favorite flick.

I missed being able to confide in Martine. I would have fantasies about being Lord High Executioner in *The Mikado* and doing away with those ''who never would be missed.'' My list was her list. My enemies were her enemies. I could talk about imaginary mayhem and murder and Martine would understand. If ever I killed anyone, I knew Martine would help me bury the body.

I realized I was alone. I had no real friends, nobody who loved me for what I was, warts and all. My children loved me, but I needed more than a child's love, after all.

I had nobody to whom I could say *Help me* if I needed help. My friend Jim O'Donnell was good company if I wanted a good time, and nothing more. My brother, to whom I had always felt close, never sensed my needs or my agony. He hadn't been glad for me when I had been happy with Martine.

Martine had very good friends. They would keep in daily contact with her. The celebrated each other's triumphs and happiness, and suffered for each other. When Martine's mother was sick, Martine's friends had visited in the hospital; with or without Martine there, they kept her mother company and tried to cheer her up. One of Martine's friends even offered to help pay the hospital costs.

Martine inspired loyalty. I realized she gave it without counting, and without reservation. She had given it to me, and I hadn't responded even though it was what I wanted and needed. Martine could inspire love. She did with me, and I had lost it or thrown it away. I still didn't remember what caused our breakup, but I knew then it had to have been me.

I didn't even know where Martine went—California or Mexico? She had friends in both places. I figured that she'd have to come back to New York. She hadn't given up her apartment. Then I thought, what if she were home?

I called her apartment, and as I expected, there was no answer. I was disappointed. Nevertheless, I kept calling her apartment almost every hour for several days hoping someone, anyone, would answer so that I could find out where Martine was. In desperation I called some of her friends, but they couldn't—or wouldn't—tell me. I decided to write to her—I figured her friends were forwarding her mail.

Dear Martine,
   Plato once tried to explain the act of sex, and opined

that man and woman were once one body. But they had become separated into two. Sexual relations, he said, is the act of trying to make one body again out of two. I have found that sex can't make one out of two, but love makes an awfully good try.

Ever since I met you I have been changing. And even with you gone, I still continue to change. But not to a different form or shape, a tadpole into a frog or a caterpillar into a butterfly. Instead, picture a peony. A tight, closed-up ball in its early stages. Then it begins to mature. Bugs are crawling all over it, then it blooms and blossoms and the bugs disappear.

I don't believe any woman can really change a man, not even you, with your great loving powers. But I know now I never needed changing. I simply was that tight ball with the bugs crawling over me, feeding off me, when we met. That's how I had been existing. But it was not me, mature, ripe. I didn't know it, but you did. I never changed. You revealed me, uncovered me.

As we lived together and loved together, the ball became larger and the bugs kept dropping off. But the process was interrupted because there were more bugs than we knew. They were tenacious, stubborn and pernicious, and enjoyed feeding off me.

I ask you to come home and finish your job. I need your nourishment and care. I need watering and tender conversation. I promise you the biggest, most brilliant flowering peony you ever saw. One that will give joy and light. One that will inspire kindness, love, and poets for generations to come.

Come home and marry me. You owe it to me. You owe it to yourself. You owe it to the world.

Come home and let us raise more peonies.

Come home. I love you.
Come home. I need you.
Come home or I shall wither and die.
Come home and we can be one.
        All the love of a wilting peony,
        Andy

I posted the letter to her New York address and waited. Then I began to call her apartment several times a day. I tried burying myself in my work and it helped, but not enough.

About two weeks after I wrote the letter I called Martine's apartment just before I went out to lunch. This had become my routine. And this time she answered.

"Hi. Did you get my letter?"

"Yes."

"Is that why you came home?"

"Yes."

"May I see you now?"

"Yes."

"Stay there. I'll be right over."

I rushed out of the office leaving word I would not return that day because of a personal emergency, and ran to Central Park. I went crazy looking for a balloon vendor. When you want one they're never around. I finally found one just setting up his stand. I had him blow up a dozen of his brightest to the biggest size possible. As I left the park with the balloons I realized I would never get them in a cab. They were huge.

I finally stopped one driver who for ten dollars agreed to let me ride and let the balloons hang out the window. He drove slowly and carefully so the balloons wouldn't get blown away. I had a tight grip on the strings of the balloons and had them wrapped around my fist as well. Still, I was afraid I was going to be yanked out of the cab by the pull. But I would not let go.

The balloons were even too large for the elevator in Martine's apartment house. I managed to get them all in, but I had to persuade another passenger to get out and wait for the next elevator.

I knocked on Martine's door. She opened it immediately. She must have been waiting for the knock. She stood there, holding that large, ridiculous, giant-sized red paper rose in her two hands, sniffing it as though it were real.